"In *Night Watch*, Gillian Wigmore's ██████████████████████
stand at the edges of lives they've al████ █████, ████████████
could be, reaching across the boundaries of time and distance
toward remembered intimacy, allowing themselves room to
wonder, grieve and imagine more. Veterinary medicine threads
through *Night Watch*: think James Herriot crossed with a gothic
Canadian sensibility. There's gore, sex, and gentleness; close calls,
strange alliances, softening bodies; bruises and blood. Wigmore's
sentences sing: clear, surprising, and delightful. The writing is as
bracing as the changing seasons in rural British Columbia, where
much of the suite is set. Wigmore takes us outside, outdoors, in all
weathers, and inside, into the secret lives of domesticated animals,
their suffering and pleasures a mirror for the confusion of our own."

— CARRIE SNYDER, AUTHOR OF *GIRL RUNNER*

"First of all: not one, but three novellas featuring veterinarians and
the people who love them? Genius! And then: the beauty of them,
the exquisitely rendered inner lives of complicated people, the
complicated workings of calves inside cows, the world in a donkey's
eye. *Night Watch* is tender and unflinching and totally captivating.
I loved it."

—ANNE FLEMING, AUTHOR OF *GAY DWARVES OF AMERICA*

"Rural veterinarians work tirelessly to save and heal what they can,
and let go of what they can't, as their spouses, siblings and lovers try
to make sense of the world blazing around them in night skies full
of stars, blistering in sunlight off snow. Characters orbit each other,
childhoods are lost and recovered, regrets owned and released,
choices made and questioned. In prose both blunt and nuanced,
brutal and tender at once, Wigmore's *Night Watch* will make you
ache for paths not taken at the same time as you relish the journeys
these characters haul you along on. You'll feel the swelter of an
awkward afternoon with a new lover, and the fatigue of a late spring
night birthing calves as though they were your own memories.
Night Watch moves with a warm, bloody, big heart that you'll carry
with you long after the last page is turned."

—LAISHA ROSNAU, AUTHOR OF *LITTLE FORTRESS*

NIGHT WATCH

The Vet Suite

Gillian Wigmore

Invisible Publishing
Halifax & Prince Edward County

Library and Archives Canada Cataloguing in Publication

Title: Night watch / Gillian Wigmore.

Names: Wigmore, Gillian, 1976- author.

Description: Three novellas.

Identifiers: Canadiana (print) 20200395289
Canadiana (ebook) 20200395955
ISBN 9781988784588 (softcover)
ISBN 9781988784724 (HTML)

Classification: LCC PS8645.I34 N54 2021 | DDC C813/.6—dc23

Edited by Leigh Nash
Cover and interior design by Megan Fildes | Typeset in Laurentian
With thanks to type designer Rod McDonald

Printed and bound in Canada

Invisible Publishing | Halifax & Prince Edward County
www.invisiblepublishing.com

Published with the generous assistance of the Canada Council for the Arts, the Ontario Arts Council, and the Government of Canada.

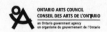

For rural vets
and those who love them.

And you are still on the highway. There are no
houses, no farms. Across the median, past the swish and thud
of the northbound cars, beyond the opposite fences,
the fields, the
climbing escarpment, solitary in the
bright eye of the sun the
birches dance, and they
dance. They have
their reasons. You do not know
anything.
Cicadas call now, in the darkening swollen air there is dust
in your nostrils; a
kind of laughter; you are still on the highway.

— from "400: coming home," dennis lee, *nightwatch*

LOVE, RAMONA

SUNFLOWERS

In the south of France in 1996, Louie and Ramona rode a bus from the holiday park to a small town twenty minutes away. It was a break from the other travellers, whose garbage littered the kitchen and lounge of the park, whose noisy gatherings filled the common spaces, and whose tents surrounded theirs in the campsite.

The speed of the bus pressed Ramona's body flat against the seatback. The heat caused an unpleasant suction between the bare skin of her thighs and the orange vinyl seats and, although they sat side by side, she was careful not to touch Louie; she kept her face turned to the window watching the green and yellow countryside zip past. He kept his eyes on the book in his lap.

Ramona chewed her lower lip. Her head kept knocking into the window when the bus roared around a corner but she didn't care. She hurt down there—her vagina was sore. It throbbed with every heartbeat. She found it hard to think of anything else. She and Louie had had sex for the first time the night before, and she was upset that she felt so upset—she was sure she wasn't supposed to feel like this.

The bus slowed beside a stone inn and stopped a few metres beyond it. Louie stowed his book in his pack, stood, and hoisted it to his back. He started off the bus, then turned back to see if she was following him. She was. They collided and both stumbled down the aisle and out of the bus into the glaring late afternoon sun.

Inside the inn it was cool and dark. They ordered steak and fries and beers at the bar then walked out the back door to a table with an umbrella in the courtyard. Roosters and chickens scratched in the dirt. The tables closest to the river seemed hazy and distant. Ramona sat down and set her pack on the ground beside her.

"We should have ordered water, too," she said. She fiddled with her pack strap. "Aren't you going to sit?"

Louie walked toward the far tables shading his eyes with one hand.

"Where are you going?"

"I wish we could go for a swim."

She inspected the water. The river flowed torpid and slow below the inn. Tall grasses leaned over the bank and the water was brown and opaque. It looked repulsive: wet, slimy. She would never swim in a river like that.

"Come on," she said. "Let's eat and then let's get back to the campsite."

He kept his back to her and his face toward the sluggish current. A rooster shook its feathers and wandered over.

"Look at the chickens, Mo." He made kissing noises at the rooster nearest him.

"That's how you call a cat," she said.

He kept up his kissing. It irritated her.

She peered in the door of the inn to see if their meal was coming, then opened her purse and dug around, but she kept an eye on Louie. He was intent on the rooster. Although everything in the courtyard was dusty and sun-faded, the rooster's feathers were deeply blue and iridescent. The rooster began a deep-throated, quiet calling: bwwwwwwooooock, bwoock, bwock. It sounded almost like purring, or maybe like some sort of sonar. She imagined that chickens and roosters had bad eyesight and compensated for it by sounding out the distance like bats. Then she thought of Louie in the dark of the tent the night before—how she felt his hand hovering over her before he touched her. The dark was so complete she couldn't see him, but his breathing filled the tent. She felt the heat coming off him and thought she might remember that her whole life. That and the sudden give, when he lay his whole weight on her and finally broke through the membrane they'd learned about in sex ed—when his penis went in all the way and she'd gasped, shocked by the pain.

The rooster bobbed his head and bwocked louder. The chickens stopped scratching and pecking and watched.

"Mona," Louie whispered. "Mona, look. I think something's going to happen."

Ramona peered into her purse. She didn't care about the chickens. She wanted lip balm or a nail file or an Aspirin—something curative, or distracting, at least.

The chickens scattered as the server bustled out of the dark doorway. She placed the glasses of beer onto the concrete table and went back inside. Ramona scowled at the beer. Beads of condensation slid down the glass.

"Louie, I don't even like beer very much."

He picked up his glass and downed most of it in one go. "You'll like this beer. It's French. Fancier than Canadian beer. It's cold, too."

"I wish you wouldn't..."

"Look at that field!" he interrupted, pointing across the river.

"What?"

"It's all sunflowers."

"So?"

"So, *sunflowers*, Mo." He sat down next to her and put his arm around her.

Her eyes flooded with tears.

"I mean," he stammered, "look around you. The *South of France*," he stage-whispered.

"Louie," she said, "my *vulva* hurts. I don't like beer. I'm not interested in roosters and I don't know what the hell book you were reading that was so interesting on the bus."

Louie made *keep it down* motions with his hands.

"Don't you shush me!" she shouted, but she shushed. "Louie," she said, and stopped. She was going to ask him to tell her three good things but she didn't. Instead she started to cry.

"Please, don't. Come on."

She glared at him. Then she plucked his hand off her arm. She blew her nose into a ratty Kleenex she'd found in her purse.

The server came back with their steaks and fries. She set the plates down with a clunk and walked away. She returned a third time with silverware, and they unwrapped their knives and forks from the cloth napkins.

The chickens and roosters crowded in again, pecking and scrutinizing, stretching their necks forward, high-stepping in slow motion until they surrounded the table, busy eating their own invisible dinner while she and Louie ate theirs. Across the river, cows skirted the sunflower field and moved down to the water to drink. Cooler air crept up from the bank. They drank their beer and picked at their food and slowly the chickens circled them and the sun sank lower in the sky.

The shadow of their table stretched far out to one side. The attached shadow of the umbrella, attached to the table's shadow, made Ramona think of walking down the road as a child, holding hands with her father, and how their shadows had stretched out impossibly long and thin ahead of them. She wasn't that young in the memory; she'd held her dad's hand until she was eleven or twelve.

She was twelve when she met Louie. They were neighbours. She was almost too old to play with him the way they did, wrestling and exploring and biking to the corner store to buy comics and ten-cent candy, but in the summer before

8

their first year of high school, they were manic about play. They played like crazy: digging a trench in Ramona's backyard so deep they could both stand upright in it; building Lego; playing Indiana Jones and gold miners; jumping off high things until one of them got hurt.

Louie, new to Finmoore, didn't know the grotty, awful parts of the town, so she showed him.

"The man who lives here tells kids he'll give them candy then he gets them to take off their shirts so he can take pictures."

Louie stared at the house through the hugely overgrown lilac hedge, breathing loudly. She watched for his reaction.

"Boys or girls?" he whispered.

"Both," she whispered back, and they stayed as long as they could by the broken fence, goosebumped and enthralled, before they ran away.

They walked their bikes down the path to the river. Willows grew so thick there they had to push the branches aside to get through. Louie said he was impressed that she went down there on her own—it was dark, and wasn't she afraid?

"Of what?" she asked. They'd settled on the bank above the river.

"I don't know."

"Name three things," she said.

"Three what?"

"Three things that scare you."

"Black holes. Spontaneous combustion. And..." he thought hard and came up short. "And penetrative sex," he finished.

"What is that?"

Louie didn't know. All he knew was the phrase from a pamphlet he'd seen on his brother's desk. He described it for her but it grossed them both out—it was called *Molestation and You*. Louie couldn't tell her what "molestation" meant.

The word made her think of rodents and the dark soil in her dad's garden after he'd broken the earth with the rototiller.

They watched the water sweep past, eating away at the bank underneath them. She looked at him and thought something she hadn't about anyone ever before: *he is important and this is something I'll remember forever*. She ran her eyes over his stretched-out sweatshirt and the sun freckling down through the trees on both of them, soaking it all in.

She was a serious, tough girl who ran as fast as the boys and had no compunction about walloping them if they irritated her. She was weepy about the deaths of pets in the books she read and romantic about what kind of woman she'd grow up to be. She was shy with adults and disdainful of kids, but in that moment, she made a decision. She leaned over and kissed Louie's cheek. He was so startled he almost slipped off the bank and fell in the river. He recovered and kissed her back, and afterwards that's what they did. With gusto. Play was forgotten—they walked and talked and kissed; they replaced digging and jumping with finding spots to make out. They wended their way through underbrush, abandoned their bikes to sit by the river, and they kissed and kissed and kissed, testing it out, tonguing around until they each knew the ridges on the soft palate of the other's mouth as well as they knew their own.

Ramona liked how kissing smelled. Louie liked how it tasted. They compared notes. When school started in September they'd spent so much time together they were ripe for some sort of falling out. Two things undid them: another kid, and Louie's father announcing his next job transfer.

"You're a jerk, Louie!" she shouted at him from the top of the slide. "Don't you even come up here! Go home!" She was scrunched up between the metal safety bars. "Go home! Go hang out with those boys if I'm so stupid!"

Louie put his hands on the railings of the slide's ladder. "You're not stupid, Mo. I never said that!"

"Brent Anderson said you did."

"*He's* stupid. I did not."

She sat down with her back to the slide, facing him. Her eyes were puffy and sore and her hair was a stringy mess from the fistfight she'd just won. Brent Anderson would have a black eye. Her new school jeans were smeared with mud and ripped on one knee.

She peered over the slide at the top of Louie's head and saw what the other kids saw: the new boy at school, black-haired and blue-eyed; a good-looking kid with the necessary mystery to be cool, a leader. She tried to see him the way she had a day earlier, when they'd hiked four kilometres to a lake to fish with cocktail shrimp stolen from his mother's fridge: hers alone, dirty-faced and mud-splattered. From high up on the slide she could feel herself become what the other kids saw when they looked at her: a bookish girl covered in freckles and fine red hair who didn't care about music or who liked whom. Even her shoes were wrong—she wore elementary kid sneakers with sproingy pink laces and they were about to start high school. She wiped her nose with her sleeve. She didn't care. She only cared about Louie. "Why are you going?"

"I have to. My whole family's going. I don't even want to."

"But why France?"

"I don't know. It's an international school? He says he can't pass it up." Louie sat down on the first rung of the ladder. She could see his black sneakers—they were cool enough, she thought. Nobody would tease him.

"How long are you going for?"

"Probably forever," he said and started to cry.

She watched him curiously. She'd never seen him cry. He cried totally differently than she did—he tried to stop it, gulping and shaking, and hold it in. She sat among the fist-sized rocks she'd collected to throw at him, then she rolled them down the slide, one by one. The noise they made was terrific. She slid down the slide after the rocks and came around beside him. She tugged him to standing and hugged him tight. "I'll write to you. I promise."

By Christmas he was gone.

Six years after their first meeting, they faced this meal together: they cut the steak and clear, red juice oozed out to the edges of the plate. The fries at the bottom of the pile soaked it up. Ramona used the huge serrated knife to shear through the meat. She forked it into her mouth where it melted in salt and blood on her tongue. It might have been the most beautiful thing she'd ever eaten. The fries were long and light yellow, peppered and salted. Louie ate fry after fry. He dug into his steak. They ate and didn't speak and the steak was heavy and gorgeous and grilled so black flecks of charred meat speckled their lips and the rims of their beer glasses.

They'd come to France so he could show her where he'd lived. His family had moved back to Canada after three years, but east, to Ottawa, and this was the first time the two of them had reunited as adults. It wasn't going as well as she'd hoped—there were gaps in what they knew about each other. The intimacies they'd had through the letters and tapes turned out to have little relevancy in the waking world, and though they knew small parts of each other inside out, there were larger parts that were too mysterious for the other to figure out. Why, for instance, was it so difficult for Ramona to get from one place to another? She was constantly losing her purse, or misplacing her passport or traveller's cheques inside it. She'd left her entire backpack in the washroom of a train station and Louie had chased a woman to get it back. But then, why was Louie so distant? Ramona couldn't figure that out at all—how was it that she knew every note of every song he'd loved between the ages of thirteen and seventeen, and now his thoughts were totally unavailable to her. The whole two weeks she'd felt confounded—nothing she'd imagined about the trip matched up with reality, but this moment, the food, made her almost forgive the mismatch.

They each leaned back from the table, lethargic and full, the red smears on their plates the only vestige of the meal. Louie pulled out his book and began to read. She dug in her purse again and grabbed a hairbrush. They'd been travelling long enough she'd lost the sense that personal hygiene belonged only in the bathroom—she'd seen a woman undress completely to wash at a water pump beside the campsite office where a couple played cards at the counter. She brushed her long hair with slow strokes. She was calm now that she'd eaten. She watched the cows roaming slowly on the far side of the river.

There was no telling where they'd be in ten years, or even fifteen. She rolled the thought over in her mind—would they have grey hair? At what age did people go grey? She pulled her tangled hairs out of the brush and dropped them on the ground. The rooster sidled up and inspected the red scribble in the dust.

"Louie," she whispered. "Look at the rooster."

He glanced up from his book. The rooster pecked at the ball of hair. One strand came up in his beak and the small mass of hair jumped up like a living thing. The rooster startled but didn't let go, so the ball swung and bopped against his breast. The rooster jumped again and the hair ball swung and the rooster spread his wings and flapped like a mad thing all around the courtyard. Dust and chickens rose in flurries. Shiny white and blue feathers scattered on the wind stirred up by the chickens and the sun was muted in the cloud of dust. The bwocking and squawking dinned around Ramona and Louie until the rooster dashed off around the side of the inn, the chickens scrabbling in his wake.

The innkeeper and the waitress watched the mayhem from the doorway. Louie and Ramona laughed until tears streaked their dusty faces. The two of them laughed until she begged to him stop, saying she would pee if they didn't, she would pee her pants.

They caught their breath eventually. They snickered and tried to breathe normally. She pulled a pack of wet wipes out of her purse and they wiped their faces. They were tired. It was getting late; bus service had ended and they'd have to walk back to the holiday park. The chickens pecked and scuffled their way back around the side of the building and slowly descended the river bank.

Louie stood and shrugged his backpack on. "Do you think we should get a bottle of wine?"

She looked at him goose-eyed. "If you think that's what it would take to get me into bed with you again, you're mistaken."

He crinkled his nose at her to make her smile. "I was kind of hoping," he said, and she did smile, a little bit.

"Maybe one bottle."

He helped her on with her pack. When she turned around she leaned against his chest and he put his arms around her and her bag. They watched the sunflowers, the swallows swooping low over the river, and the river flowing below the bank.

"I just didn't know it would hurt so much," she said after a while.

"I'm sorry, Mo."

"You should have stayed with me."

"I thought you were coming out. When those guys from Israel got home from the bar I heard them, and I didn't think... I just wanted to join in."

They hugged and Ramona watched the willow branches draped in the water bob in the current. She waited.

"I should have stayed," he said, finally, and she smiled, but the feeling of satisfaction didn't last.

They went into the inn and each paid for their meal, then walked out onto the road that would lead them back to the park. The low light of early evening was filtered as if through a dirty glass. Ramona took Louie's hand and it was hot and dry. They moved together and it was so familiar to Ramona, like the smell of her own breath.

PAPAYAS

In the fall of 2002, at Nadi International Airport in Fiji, Ramona and her fiancée Charlie Dearly, of the silly name (she knew she'd get used to it eventually), stepped off the plane into a sauna. Her hair stuck to her neck and to her clammy face. Charlie was sweaty and anxious, his blond hair plastered to his head, his fair skin red with heat. He peered ahead, past the Fijians queuing up to go into the terminal.

"Come on," he urged, but she couldn't. She walked slowly, like she was pushing against a current. Once they were inside the building, she gazed up at the offices ringing a second-floor balcony. The room was bright, echoing with the voices of hundreds of people and the wheels of rolling luggage, and birds flew in and out of the breeze-block windows. There were hardly any walls. Ramona stared up at the space sprawling above the lineups of people inching through security. The air bulged and swam. She wondered if she was having a stroke. Charlie took her arm. She tried to focus on his eyes, but they were big and then small. She laughed at him and he shook her.

"Jesus, Ramona. Come on."

Her fingers hurt, crushed in his—the ring he'd given her dug into her flesh as he pulled her along. She slipped out of his grasp. "What's the hurry?"

He didn't answer. They crossed the room, weaving between piles of bags, baskets, plants, people fanning themselves, and pulled up short in front of a travel agent's counter.

A huge woman in a rose-coloured muumuu laughed when she saw them. Ripples flowed down her rolls of fat. She talked to them in a loud voice, but no matter how hard she tried to concentrate, Ramona could not understand what was being said. She watched, agog, as the woman's lips flapped, her white teeth shining in her mouth. Ramona wondered what was wrong with her brain—she thought back to the plane. She'd felt sick, she remembered, and hadn't wanted to eat; her stomach was upset. Charlie had given her some motion-sickness tablets that she'd eyed suspiciously before taking, but he was a doctor, sort of—a vet—and it was medicine for humans, so she took it. That's what had made her brain so spongy. She tried again to focus on the conversation happening in front of her. Charlie was giving the woman his Visa, so something must have been decided.

"Green Bay Resort?" he asked.

"*Green* Bay *Resort*," the woman corrected, smiling and zipping his card through her machine.

Ramona pulled out a hair tie and started to do her hair. It felt so good to slick it back with the sweat from her temples, squeezing it into a ponytail then twisting it into a bun. She had no idea how involved she was in the process until Charlie barked her name, startling her. "The taxi's waiting."

The travel agent waved them off, still laughing.

Outside, back in the sun, the heat made her want to lie down. Charlie stuffed her into a taxi. It had no inner door panels and Ramona could see the workings of the door handles, the silver couplings, bolts, ratchets. Charlie shoved her over, sat down beside her and set their packs upright on the seat between them like two extra passengers.

He directed the driver to a marina on the other side of Lautoka. The taxi took off like a slapped horse and hurtled down the road, slowing only minimally at armoured checkpoints where soldiers with machine guns waved and smiled as they drove past.

"Why do those men have guns?" she asked. She thought

Charlie would probably know. He seemed very much in charge here in Fiji.

"The coup," the driver said, grinning into the rearview mirror. "It's the coup. Lots of soldiers right now, but lots of tourists, too!" He shook his finger to make that point.

"There's been a coup?"

"Only a little one," the driver said, showing a centimetre of space between his brown thumb and the pink pad of his pointer finger. "No problem."

They sped past a truck full of goats and another full of people. Farmland slid past too quickly to register anything but the fluorescence of the green crops in neat rows. Charlie stared out the window and Ramona tried to keep her head still, but the taxi went so fast her eyes ping-ponged back and forth trying to keep up.

They lurched to a stop at the marina. The teal blue ocean stretched out before them. On either side of the concrete breakwater small- and medium-sized boats bobbed at their moorings: red and yellow boats, boats with oars, and boats with tiny motors, all full of people. There was so much noise from the motors and the people talking Ramona wanted to hold her hands over her ears. Charlie made her stand with their packs as he went to talk to a man holding a sign that said Green Bay Resort. The taxi honked and roared away. She pushed the packs over and sat on them. She felt a mess. Not how she'd planned to look and feel when she saw Louie again. She drew up her knees and folded her head to rest on them.

She remembered the early part of their separation, hers and Louie's, as a strange, quiet time. After reading and riding her bike, writing to Louie was what Ramona spent most of her time doing. At first, their letters were full of drawings and goofy messages, anecdotes about family and full of hopes that they'd see each other again soon. After the winter passed and spring crept by, muddy and slow, the letters got more introspective. They were thirteen then, and thinking about more serious things—why movies always ended so sappy, what it meant when their parents weren't talking to each other, how to feel about death if you didn't believe in God. The letters were a place they put their big questions—they didn't have many answers between the two of them, but it helped to share.

For his fourteenth birthday, Louie got a tape recorder. Ramona got fewer letters after that; instead, he sent cassette tapes of the music he listened to. Mixtapes, at first full of songs he dubbed off his parents' albums, until he started to discover and then share his own favourites. Played on repeat back in Canada, they became Ramona's favourites, too: strange French pop songs that no one else in her classes had heard of, B-sides of Beatles songs, reggae, early punk. Sometimes Louie prefaced the songs with talking—Ramona could hear his voice say the name of the song and what he'd been doing when he'd first heard it or who had introduced him to it. She listened to him breathing with her heart tight, waiting for him to say something important. He rarely did. She listened for it anyway.

Ramona had a key for her family's post office box. It was her job to stop after school and pick up the mail, and if there was a parcel from France, she wouldn't get home until suppertime. She had a Walkman, and listening to the tapes, walking down by the river, was as close as she could be to Louie's thoughts. The tapes were like a rope she held in one hand all the way through high school, and the letters she wrote in response to them made her feelings more understandable to herself. It wasn't kissing or fishing, but it was pretty good.

Today. She would see him again today. Ramona startled awake feeling blistered. She'd dozed off. She sat up and took in the boats and the ocean and felt a headache bang to life at the base of her skull. Charlie came up with two bottles of water.

"You should be wearing your hat."

She took a bottle of water and drank most of it before trying to speak. "Where are we?" Her tongue felt enormous in her mouth.

"We're waiting for a boat to take us to the resort."

She peered at him. "Are you sure about this resort? It's the one Louie said?"

He snorted. "I hope so. You weren't much help back there. You were too out of it to contribute."

"Thanks to your pills."

"Feeling better?"

She scowled and drank more.

He inspected the boats then pointed. "That's the one. It'll be an hour to the west islands."

The water made her feel better. She leaned over and put her head on his shoulder.

He shook his head. "I can't believe we're here. What a stupid idea."

She was stung. "Travelling together before the wedding is a good test. I read it in that marriage book."

"Not everything you read is true," he said. "And meeting up with your ex-boyfriend and his girlfriend for a holiday is idiotic."

"He's not my ex-boyfriend. He's my oldest friend. And it's too late for complaining." She found her sunglasses in her purse, put them on, and turned away to end the conversation.

When their time came to get on the boat, Charlie helped her up and they gathered their packs. He chose their seats on one of the long benches that lined the little cabin. It was easy to follow him, to carry on as if they hadn't argued. It's what she'd been doing since they'd met again, years after they'd shared the stage in a high school production of *Carousel*. She'd had a background role—he, two years older than she, had played the lead.

She'd been in a liminal state then. At university, while the girls in her dorm all seemed to be studying organic chemistry or kinesiology, she'd ground to a halt; university was not like it seemed in the pamphlets. She did an aimless year of sociology, philosophy and psychology, and spent a lot of time in the TV lounge. In psychology she often heard people talking about wanting to teach, and so she followed that crowd across campus and finished up her degree with a minor in psych and a major in education. It was easy to get on the substitute teacher list at her old high school when she returned home from school in the spring. It was easy, too, to take the job they offered her when she finished, even if it was in PE—there would be an opening in social studies soon enough, they said. So Ramona found herself living in an apartment down the street from her parents, her work wardrobe composed of sweatpants and school T-shirts, trying to pass as a grownup.

Charlie Dearly lived downstairs. His trim physique hadn't changed since high school. His sense of humour hadn't changed, either. He gave her a wolf-whistle the first time he saw her in the building's foyer. She laughed in response, but there was relief in it—doubt had begun to creep in when she found herself slumping into the dumpy chair in her little apartment night after night. A postcard of Louie's from Nashville describing a gig with a country music star whose name she recognized had made her pause and examine her second-hand chairs and desk. She'd stared at the box of silver tea things her mum had dropped off that neither of them had any use for. When Charlie called out her name after he whistled at her, it was easy for her to stop and wait for him.

Charlie loved catching Ramona up on what he'd been doing for the past eight years. Their dates at the local pub, or the rodeo, had an ironic, kitschy appeal for her—he bought her cotton candy and an imitation silver belt buckle with a bronc rider on it—and there was a rudderless appeal to going to the local movie theatre or out for dinner at the restaurant her parents had taken her to as a little girl. The stuffed fox she'd loved still stood poised near the kitchen's swinging door, dusty and wild; her father had always let her stroke its glassy eye.

Charlie knew a lot about taxidermy. He could tell her when an animal was posed unnaturally by the stretch of fur over its artificial bones. His vet practice was well-established. He'd bought it from the retiring vet who'd been there for forty years. Charlie's reputation may have been question-able—rumour had it he took his time getting out to farms when called, and she'd heard an old fellow at the bakery say that "young Dr. Dearly interrupts!" Charlie didn't care what anyone said. He was going to buy the property next door to his clinic and build a house. That lit a slow fuse in Ramona. She'd always loved playing house.

It surprised her that Charlie didn't seem to like animals. In the early days of their relationship, she went with him on a farm call to see some calves with pasture poisoning. It happened while he was cleaning up: she saw him punch a Holstein in the head. The cow seemed unfazed. It poked its nose right back into the case where Charlie kept his meds and tools, so he punched it again in the ear. Ramona flinched. The cow shook her head, snot and drool flying, and Charlie told it to fuck off. Then he noticed Ramona watching.

"It's not like they really feel it, babe. Well, they do, I mean, they have nerve endings. Smacking a cow is like talking to someone really far away—the message gets to them slowly. You have to yell, wave your arms or something. Exaggerate. I'm not being mean when I hit the cow, I'm just getting my message across." The cow's enormous wet nose smeared a snail path up Ramona's arm and she shrieked. Charlie laughed and two-handed the cow to get her to move on.

"See? It's like she's on the moon and we're yelling at her about the weather on Earth."

He'd pulled Ramona close, despite his poop-smeared coverall, and kissed her. He slid his hand down her back until it cupped her butt cheek and whispered in her ear just the right dirty things to make her blush. He laughed and they packed up his gear and drove away from the farm together.

Charlie liked the puzzle of vet medicine; he liked that you could take an animal apart and put it back together. And, he explained to her once while she sipped a gin and tonic, watching him operate late at night in his clinic while the ice melted in the drink waiting for him next to the sink, it didn't matter how badly you sewed if you were a vet—if you pulled the stitches tight and put enough in there, the wound stayed closed. He didn't leave nice scars, Charlie, but he was thorough. A loud laugher, a wild ride, and a good enough vet, as he'd put it.

Charlie bought her flowers on Fridays and let her choose the curtains and the bedspread. He didn't care who they hung out with, as long as there was beer and music and lots going on. Ramona was surprised when he told her he'd spent a term as president of the Canadian Veterinary Medicine Association—it seemed an important position and Charlie was a little abrupt, a little off sometimes. It was hard for Ramona to picture him presiding over a meeting, but he prized getting through an agenda at lightning speed, the same way he prized a quiet operating theatre and clean instruments when a dog with a compound femur fracture was on the table before dinner: Charlie Dearly got things done, and Ramona knew this because he told her. It was a chief topic of his conversation. She didn't mind—it impressed her slightly and gave her more time to herself, which she spent teaching, shopping, planning letters, and learning to bake. He made her laugh, and he wasn't bad in bed. She'd give him that.

There was magic in becoming a grownup with or without Louie. She'd always imagined doing it with him, and she'd told him all that in the letters through their teens, but in her fantasies they lived in a garret in Paris or on a houseboat on a canal in Amsterdam. With Charlie she felt like a version of an adult she could recognize: shopping at the supermarket for treats for their lunches, taking clothes to the drycleaners, making hamburgers on a summer Saturday. The postcards from Louie started to seem childish, but there was a pull in her when she read them; somewhere deep inside she felt a certain betrayal of him, but it wasn't enough to make her want to give up her engagement ring or her newly tiled bathroom. She felt she'd skipped a whole section of being a young adult, and it was this anticipation of possible regret later on that had brought her to Fiji for one last trip with Louie and his girlfriend—and with Charlie. Charlie said he understood, but he'd dropped the nonchalance before they left.

"You'd never want to be with a loser like that, though."

"Like what? You mean Louie?" She was folding laundry, setting aside the T-shirts and shorts she'd take with her.

"He doesn't even live anywhere."

"He's got an apartment in Toronto he sublets when he's on tour."

Charlie snorted. "Tour. It's not like he's famous." He picked up a pair of panties from the basket and fingered the lace. "You're not bringing these." He threw them at the dresser.

She'd laughed. "Charlie, don't be silly. It's just a trip."

Charlie left it alone but it wasn't true, that it was just a trip. Secretly, it was a test. She remembered listening to Louie's mixtapes at fifteen, lying on her bed in a tangle of magazines and blankets. She'd planned their wedding—on a beach, she thought, and she'd wear a white slip dress and leave her hair free to blow in the wind. Louie would play a song for her at a barbeque banquet. There would be fireflies.

Ramona was going to Fiji to make sure she was on the right track. What if Charlie was a mistake? She wanted to see Louie with his girlfriend, see him in a different future, so that she could carry on with this one. She was planning a church wedding for Charlie and her—she didn't have all the details finalized, but she was close.

On their way out to the island, water splashed up in the boat's wake, bathwater warm and Epsom-salty. Surrounded by other passengers draped on the benches, pressed up against their backpacks, Ramona and Charlie watched the lumpy green islands zoom past. She leaned back against him and he put his arms around her as the boat bounced into the waves. Flying fish leaped out of the water like flung spots of mercury. It was a long hour, and it felt heavy, like it mattered, each detail clear and sharp. There was nostalgia mixed in with the excitement Ramona was feeling—the green of the islands was so brilliant against the jewel-coloured sea, she felt like she was starring in the kind of home movie she'd show to her own kids someday. *And then we boated out to an island and I couldn't even imagine where we were going to land*. The tourists around them chatted, the boat's drivers laughed, but Ramona heard none of it over the roar of the motor and the sound of her own thoughts.

When they climbed onto the dock at the resort she was damp and tired and sated in the way she remembered feeling as a kid after a long day playing in the sun. The feeling didn't last. Louie and his girlfriend Jessica were waiting on the shore where they docked. Small and dark-haired, with a thin nose and a sharp chin, everything about her irritated Ramona: her sandals and her bracelets and her perfect teeth. Louie stood beside her, the same and different. He was older but still youthful in a loose white shirt, bright against the dark foliage and the mess of people on the dock.

Ramona's heart lurched. She lifted an arm to wave, bouncing on her toes, then thought better of it and stopped, but Charlie had seen. His eyebrows drew together. Ramona tried to collect herself, but Louie in the flesh made her dizzy.

Charlie took Louie's proffered hand and shook it. They wore false smiles that Ramona and Jessica mimicked during their brief, false hug. They stood back and stared at each other and Ramona knew, as the sick feeling returned to her guts, that Charlie was right—this was a mistake.

"Let's get a drink," Jessica said.

Ramona shot her a look of gratitude and was surprised to see it returned with a smile, and she felt warmed. She fell into step with Jessica. The women led the way off the dock and left the men to carry the packs.

It was a resort only by the loosest definition of the word. There were ten little wood-and-grass huts surrounded by tall coconut trees, and a bar off the central dining room—but the dining room's floor was sand and the bar served only Kingfisher beer in one-litre bottles.

As the sun dipped into the ocean, Ramona, Louie, Charlie, and Jessica chose a table near the bar and waited for the awkward part to end. Mosquitoes buzzed around their faces, touching down on sticky skin and taking off before the blow landed. Laughter from the other tables filled the room. They sat and watched each other and Ramona wondered how it would be here—were there waiters? Would someone bring them water? Jessica leaned over and whispered to Louie, then she stood and excused herself and left.

"She's going to the toilet," he said.

"Where is it?" Ramona was in pretty desperate need, but she wondered if it would be weird if she followed Jessica. What would they say to each other over the sinks? The headache she'd had back in Lautoka bloomed in her forehead.

"They're behind this building," Louie said. "I checked them out. Concrete. Full of geckos, but they flush."

Ramona stood, then thought better of it. She could brave the small talk in the bathroom, but what would Louie and Charlie say to each other while she was gone? They were both so stiff and gruff—Louie fumbling a pack of cigarettes out of his pocket, Charlie glaring at him while he did it. Then Charlie shoved back his chair and stood up.

"I'll find a light."

Ramona sat back down in surprise. Charlie went over to the bar, but when no one came to help him, he reached over and filched a lighter from among the glasses. He came back to the table and lit the cigarette hanging out of Louie's mouth. Louie held the pack up to him. Charlie took one and lit his own, then he sat back down. Both men exhaled, then looked at Ramona. She stood abruptly and left for the bathroom. Their two sets of eyes on her were too much.

She was so hot and so cold. The sand on the concrete floors under her bare feet felt slippery. Grit was packed between her toes and she leaned against the wall with one hand to wipe off her foot. A little girl, maybe two years old, shuffled across the passageway ahead of her. She wore an adult's black flip flops and took slow, short steps to keep them on her feet. Her head was down, concentrating. Ramona smiled.

"Hey there," she said.

The girl stopped and whipped her head around at the sound. She narrowed her eyes at Ramona and sniffed twice. Then she growled deep in her throat.

Ramona caught her breath, blushing furiously. The girl trudged on and Ramona looked around in case anyone had seen. Jessica stood at the end of the passageway.

"The bathroom isn't so bad," she said as she passed. "But I hope you brought your own toilet paper."

When Ramona got back to the table, Louie and Charlie each had a hand wrapped around a half-finished beer and Jessica was sipping from another. An unopened bottle sat sweating at her place. Full bowls steamed, untouched, in front of each of them.

"Curry," Charlie said.

"Fish." Louie peered at his. "I think."

Jessica said something Ramona didn't catch that both men found funny. She felt ten steps behind. She sat down on the edge of her chair. "It's too hot for curry."

Around them the other guests ate and talked and laughed and drank, and at their table Jessica and Charlie clinked glasses, Louie downed the rest of his beer, and Ramona felt the night slip away. She felt the three of them pull together without her and it was unbearable. She stretched her neck to try and get cool air into her lungs, but couldn't. The room blurred into a soup. She swooned, or thought she did—her head swam and the earth lurched, but she didn't faint. She gripped the edge of the table, gritted her teeth. Said, "I'm actually not very hungry. I'll see you later." And she stood and walked out into the dark, windy world outside the bar.

Ramona had had two fever dreams as a child that she re-membered. One was violent and dark—like being a toddler amongst the legs of grownups in a department store on a sale day, full of threatening brown and purple shapes lurching at and past her. The other was worse: she'd lain on her back on her parents' bed, the pillow under her head wet from sweat or tears. Maybe she was five years old. She was staring at the white panels in the ceiling when suddenly all the grooves in the tiles smoothed out and the ceiling dipped down toward her. She couldn't scream. The ceiling got so close to her face— and then it was another face peering at her, a woman's face that bulged and swam as she struggled to get away, her limbs frozen, her voice trapped in her throat. The woman in the ceiling menaced her until she could see herself from outside her body—a tiny child in a rucked up nightgown struggling on the bed under a liquefied ceiling. Ramona remembered the glaring whiteness, the helplessness in her fear.

Walking out in the wind, blind in the darkness, she reeled and stumbled. Dead-centre in this, her third fever dream, weak and tired, she tried to see herself from above, feeling for the path with her toes, just to see anything at all. It was profoundly black after the bright lights of the bar. Every time she felt grass underfoot she bent down and ran her hand over the ground until she found gravel to determine if the path was on her left or right. She knew her eyes would adjust, but for the moment she was panicked, blind in the warm wind off the ocean somewhere in the South Pacific with no friends and nothing in her stomach. And she'd been growled at by a hostile child. She was glad she was wearing lacy panties, at least. When they found her mauled and dead and eaten by a wild pig, at least her underwear would be good.

She wiped the tears off her cheeks with one wrist. She felt so stupid. She was lost. The ocean pounded on the beach and she knew if she kept that on her left side she should run into one of the huts soon, but hadn't she gone too far? She walked stiffly, her arms out like ineffective antennae. She made her way between two trees—she could hear their huge leaves rattling and shushing far above her, but then all of a sudden, she couldn't walk anymore. A rope across her hips held her back. She put her hands down and tried to pry it off, but it held tight and grew tighter the harder she tried to push through. Suddenly it snapped and she fell down. She could just make out a white hammock swaying between two other trees a ways away. A hammock. That's what she was tangled in.

She sat on the grass and held her hot head, sick and furious. She was stuck. She couldn't go back to the bar because of pride, but she couldn't find her hut, either, and the thought of searching further in the dark made tears come to her eyes. She got to her hands and knees and crawled toward the sound of the water. At least she was still moving.

If Ramona was writing the book of her life, which she never would, she wasn't a writer—so if she was writing a letter to someone but not Louie, say to her mother or her hypothetical children—she'd write about how much the sand hurt her knees and how grateful she was for the cool night wind. She'd write how once she left the dry sand and hit the wet she stopped, turning to lay on one side facing the water, how she listened to the waves and wondered what sea animals would crawl into her hair if she kept still long enough. Normally that thought would have her up and brushing herself off, but she was so tired. She watched the waves swallow the stars and spit them out. She watched the clouds appear and disappear. She realized her eyes had adjusted and she could see. The nausea receded a bit and she thought about sitting up.

Maybe Louie would leave the table to come find her. Charlie wouldn't. He'd be having too good a time regaling Jessica with stories about himself. Louie would leave the table, saying he had to take a piss. He'd leave the bar and somehow be able to see better than she could. He'd see a body on the beach and his heart would lurch in his chest. He'd run flat out to make sure it wasn't Ramona, but it was her! He'd gather her up, say her name. He'd brush her sweaty hair off her forehead, make sure she was breathing. He'd kiss her gently. He'd slide the strap off her collarbone and kiss her there. He'd kiss the divot at the base of her neck. He'd set her head gently on the sand and start unbuttoning her shirt. She could feel his fingertips fumbling with the cotton and the bone buttons. She could feel his weight on the sand beside her. She felt his hands slide her bikini top off her breasts and cup them and then she felt his mouth on her left nipple, then her right. The scent of Louie's hair was hot skin and ozone, disorienting Ramona, who associated the smell with snow. He came back up and kissed her mouth and licked her neck and moved her face this way and that. He undid the buttons on her shorts and slid them off her.

There was a second Ramona might have stopped him so she wouldn't cheat on Charlie. And then she observed herself not stopping him, not worrying, just feeling. It wasn't like her, but she didn't dwell on it—she focused on Louie's hands, his mouth. Her nipples hardened in the wind and the hair on her neck stood up as he skimmed his hand up between her thighs. Her knees jolted when he kissed her pubic hair. He moved both hands around to the backs of her thighs and pulled her closer to him. She brought her hands to his hair, feeling the heat of his scalp, the damp of his sweat at his temples.

They didn't speak at all until he said to her, "Here?"

She shook her head. Her skin was sore from the sand.

"Come with me," he said and pulled her to standing. They were naked and his cock stood out from his body, bobbing and pointing as he gathered their clothes. He took her by the hand and led her into the bushes away from the beach. She followed him, the wind brushing all parts of her body. Small cascades of sand tumbled down her skin like pixie dust, grazing the backs of her knees, trickling down her legs as it came free. He led her to the concrete shower house and the lawn behind it. They were blocked from the beach by bushes and shielded from the resort by the shower house. He sat her down and kissed her again. He pushed on her shoulder so she lay down. He hovered above her.

She reached for him.

It was darker off the beach. He was a dark shadow against a dark sky but the sensation of him inside her was vivid. She tried to stop thinking so she could just feel, but fragments crept in: the flying fish, the heat where she'd leaned against

Charlie's body on the boat and his dryer-sheet smell; the moonlight beaming through the translucent crabs on the beach, the waves; Jessica standing on the dock waving at them.

There were memories, too, of Louie in France—his calloused fingertips brushing the tips of her nipples; the time he almost knocked her out with his elbow in the tent trying to roll them both over to get on top of her.

Ramona pushed against his chest to get him off. He sat back and let her up, letting her rise and turn, then she took him by the shoulder and pushed him down so he lay on his back. She climbed on and guided his penis into her with her hand. She closed her eyes. She rode, sparks flashing in her skull, her headache dissipating. She felt the rare, leaden pull of orgasm creep up her lower half, melting her legs and ass, and she reached for it, riding hard until she came, eyes glued shut, gasping.

She dropped her chin to her chest, her bare back bowed, her sweat cooling. She imagined him bringing his hands up to stroke her sides, her cheek.

"Okay?" he'd ask. She could barely make him out on the grass beneath her.

She breathed hard, coming back to herself. There was nothing on the grass underneath her but her crumpled clothes, her own wet hands.

She got up on her knees. She groped her way to the outdoor shower. She startled when the light flicked on but the outside bulb was so weak she didn't feel she was visible. She turned the water on warm and soaped herself up. She used the yellow bar left on the shelf, lathering until a thick juice of suds streamed from her hands. She rubbed herself all over. Her face slack with mindless action.

She'd have to leave the resort in the morning. That was clear. She closed her eyes and let the water drum down on her hair. She was already gone in her mind—the boat, the taxi, the airplane, and home—she had to get back to the hut and pretend she'd been so sick that she'd had a shower, so Charlie would find her sound asleep in bed.

She woke Louie in the morning by making birdcalls outside his little hut.

"You sound like a wounded ibis."

"That's an ungulate. Or else that's an ibex. What's an ibis?"

He threw his towel at her out the window and came outside. They walked down to the dock. Jessica was still asleep. Charlie was packing up his and Ramona's hut, then he was going to pay up so they could leave.

Ramona and Louie sat on the dock on his towel, already hot in the morning sun. Louie chucked shells someone had left in a pile into the ocean. The morning was warm. Ramona pulled a tube of sunscreen out of her purse and squirted it into her hand to rub on her arms.

Louie watched her. "You missed a spot."

She gave him the tube and turned her back to him. He slipped the straps of her sundress off her shoulders and then she heard him shake the tube and squirt the cream into his hand. His first cold touch sent electricity all through her. She closed her eyes and let him rub.

"You don't have to go, Mo."

She didn't answer. She peeled the wood of the dock with her fingernail.

"Why are you going? We haven't even explored this place yet."

"We weren't going to." She thought she would change the subject. "What are three regrets you have, Lou? Name them."

"I'm not playing that game." He stopped his rubbing. She could feel his breath cool on the fresh sunscreen on her back. "Why did we come here if we weren't going to explore?" It was a reasonable question, but Ramona heard Louie's real question underneath it: *Why did you drag me here?*

She pulled up her straps. "You and Jessica can have a nice holiday at this resort and we'll carry on. I read about another island that has a volcano on it."

He threw another shell. "We could come, too."

She shook her head. Louie had knocked papayas out of the trees for breakfast. She picked up a speckled fruit and handed it to him.

He used a knife he'd grabbed from the bar to slice into the soft flesh. "When will I see you again?"

"At the wedding, I hope."

She bit into the slice of papaya he handed her and it dripped down her chin into the neck of her dress. He wiped up the drips with the palm of his open hand. She went still. Then she stood up. She had to stick with the plan: she was going to marry Charlie. After whatever nonsense that was last night, there was no telling what she might do. She shook herself and put on a bright smile for Louie. He looked so good in the morning sun, so solid and sexy. She stared out to sea and trolled her memory for something awful to erase how much she loved the feel of his hands on her body.

She remembered fireworks at a campsite near Marseilles. She'd sat with a girl from Germany on a block of concrete near the bathrooms. They'd passed a bottle of red wine between them and Ramona, when her turn came, drank quickly so she could get back to the show—she was pretty sure she was discovering something amazing about the timing of the fireworks—there was a pause between the clap of noise and the eruption of colour that seemed loaded. She felt like she'd known all along it was important, but just this instant she was coming to understand it. The girl from Germany was getting very drunk as a result of Ramona's skyward attention—it was always her turn to drink.

"There, see?" Ramona had nudged the girl's shoulder and knocked the bottle away from her lips. A red dollop landed in her lap.

"Scheisse."

"Sorry. Look up, see? Hey, Louie! You're missing the fireworks!" she'd yelled toward the bathroom.

He'd been gone ages. The other German girl had too, as a matter of fact. They'd met up at the beach near the campsite earlier and bonded over the tiny plot of sand they'd occupied among a throng of French beach-goers.

The trip down the coast of France had cost Louie and Ramona, not in currency but in intimacy. She couldn't bear to listen to him eat chips, and he was always buying chips. There'd been a whole day they didn't speak at all except to negotiate sharing the double port on his Walkman.

They'd been eager to make friends with the German girls. Ramona thought they were all about the same age and that was a pleasing commonality, but she was slightly intimidated by the fact both girls could speak five languages.

"Inge? Where are you from?"

"Cologne." She drank from the bottle and handed it to Ramona. There were two inches left. Inge smiled and delivered a slow-motion, off-kilter nudge to Ramona's shoulder that knocked the bottle out of Ramona's hand onto the sand below. The wine leaked out, staining the sand black in the dim light of the bathrooms.

"Scheisse." Ramona stared groundward.

Inge laughed. A three-tiered orange firework blasted into nothingness above them.

"Where's your friend? What's her name?"

"Laure," Inge said. "Where's your boyfriend?"

"He's not my boyfriend. He's my...boy friend."

"Yes, your boyfriend."

"Well, sort of. He's in the bathroom, I think."

"I think not."

"Pardon?"

Inge had lifted her head and gestured up the bank with her lips and chin. It was chic, Ramona thought. She wondered if she could pull off such a European gesture.

She got to her feet and stumbled up the bank in the general direction of Inge's moue. She'd drunk more than she thought, but it made her smile. When she rounded the side of the bathrooms and saw Laure on her knees in front of Louie, Louie's hands in Laure's hair, Louie's eyes two identical globes of *holy shit, Ramona*, she'd stumbled. Then she'd turned and run.

He was never a great penpal—Ramona was always the better correspondent. There were huge gaps between grades and events that he never bothered to fill in. Ramona detailed almost every day leading up to, including, and after her graduation from high school. She gave up on letters in the weeks prior to the France trip, when Louie started fielding daily phone calls about plane tickets and itineraries. Ramona was worried he'd be sick of her before she even arrived, and she probably wasn't far off, but the first time he'd hugged her when she got off the plane she was sure they both felt that same old fire light up. She'd been nurturing that spark since he'd left her when they were kids, and even if it was more imagined than real by the time she'd arrived in France.

Until she caught Louie with Laure on her knees. She ran back down the embankment, down the path to the beach, past couples and groups sitting on blankets watching the fireworks in the dark. She ran until she hit the water's edge. She breathed hard and fought the vomit in her throat. She stared at the water. She thought about throwing herself in. She didn't know what to do, then realized she was doing the same thing she'd always done—she was waiting for Louie. She swore, but she still waited a minute or two to see if he would follow her. He didn't. She faced the black Mediterranean for a moment and then she turned back the way she'd come. *No way*, she'd thought. *There is no way this is going to end it*. She'd read, and believed in, so many stories about girls with romantic destinies; how could hers be any different?

At the end of their holiday in France, Louie put her on the plane in Paris. In the airport check-in line, he'd hugged her tight. Said, *Fuck, Mo*, into her hair and she'd felt the length of his body pressed up against hers and she knew it so well. In their days together after the fireworks she'd done her best to love him every way imaginable—now his body was like a map she'd traced until she knew the contour lines off by heart. She'd absorbed him, eighteen, stringy hair and gap teeth, and she'd smiled. "Write me a letter, okay?"

He'd nodded, but he wouldn't write many after that—he discovered postcards and got mildly famous. Ramona wrote on as if nothing had changed.

In Fiji Ramona kissed Louie goodbye when no one was looking, got into the boat with Charlie, and didn't look back. Charlie loved the volcano. He loved the coastal towns they visited and the Fijian beer. He loved the boat rides and the flying fish. He swam with manta rays and dove with sharks. He loved the singing and dancing in the tiny Fijian villages and afterward, even years after they got home, he told the story of the shitty, sand-floored restaurant and the girl who'd growled at Ramona at a million staff parties and bonfires. He even referenced it in his wedding speech. Ramona regretted telling him the story, but she kept quiet. Kept her own version of things to herself.

KINGFISHERS

In 2013, in the thin light of an August morning, a Greyhound bus full of sleeping passengers pulled into the Finmoore co-op parking lot in the foothills of the Northern Rockies. Ramona leaned against her dirty Suburban, her arms wrapped around her middle, against the chill. She felt old and disheveled: hair all over the place, her jacket too big and worn, with holes at the elbows and pockets peeling off. She squinted against the dust, then went and stood on the sidewalk and waited for Louie to get off the bus.

"Ramona." He hugged her. "Are you crying?"

She swallowed. "Sorry. I do it all the time. It used to drive Charlie crazy. I can't help it. I'm a crybaby." She reached out to squeeze his arm. "I'm glad you're here. It's been so long."

"I'm sorry I didn't make it for the funeral."

"Don't worry. It feels like I missed it, too."

He turned to find his luggage. "I have my pack and a guitar case and that's all."

"Okay," she said and they were businesslike. The wind sprayed them with fine gravel as they carted his things to the truck.

She stared at him sidelong, trying to see how he'd changed since they'd seen each other last, at her wedding eleven years earlier. The wedding had been a nightmare. She'd wished at the time he hadn't come. She was pretty sure he felt the same way.

Ramona pulled the tailgate down for him.

"Nice truck."

"It was Charlie's. For work. I can't get rid of it."

"Hey, thanks for getting up so early to come and get me. I could've got a cab, you know."

She pushed her hair out of her eyes, wiped the stragglers out of her mouth. "There are no cabs here. I'm up early anyway. I'm not sleeping very much."

He swung his bag into the back, then looked at her. She stood with one hand on the tailgate, the other holding back her hair. She watched him carefully.

"I don't need as much sleep as I used to, not like when we were teenagers." It wasn't what she wanted to say. The lines around his eyes crinkled and she could see, underneath, he was the old Louie, still the person who'd known her longest and best in the world. He hugged her. She exhaled and melted against him, and they fit, just like they always had. They stood in the parking lot in front of the Greyhound station and the pharmacy and her arms came up around him and pulled him to her. Then she really cried.

He sat at the kitchen island while she put the kettle on and ground beans for coffee. She felt his eyes on her as she moved from the fridge to the counter with the cream, from the counter to the stove as the kettle boiled. She was suddenly shy with him in her kitchen—there was unopened mail beside the fridge; papers were stacked deep on the microwave; a mess of magazines and plates covered the table. Empty tea cups lined with sedimentary rings of tannin from time she'd spent in this room coasting, trying to keep her brain in her body while the world outside went on without her, were littered on every surface, some of them overcome by the tide of papers and magazines.

When the kettle boiled and the press was pressed, she finally put a mug of coffee in front of him, he brought it to his lips and sipped, and she saw him realize she'd already put the cream in. She blushed with pride for remembering how he took his coffee. She got eggs out of the fridge and pulled a frying pan down from a high cupboard.

"What can I do to make it better, Mo?"

"You could get the toast on. The bread is on the counter."

He rolled his eyes. "You know what I mean."

She wanted to laugh, but she didn't know anymore how he could help, didn't know whether having him come had been a good idea. He drank his coffee in her and Charlie's kitchen and it made her remember how things were and how things weren't; he had a whole life without her now. She knew this, and for just a second, she panicked. "Look, I'm glad you came." She came to the island and sat down with him.

"But what, Mo?"

"I mean," she breathed out. "I don't know if I need you." She pushed her hair back from her face. She saw his jaw clench. His eyebrows draw together.

"Why did you call me then? I was on tour. I cut it short because you said you needed me."

"I need you, I do, Louie, I'm just so confused." She was sweating. What was she afraid of? Of course this was the right thing. She couldn't hesitate. A thin gold chain hung around her neck, long enough so that it dipped into the v of her sweater. She played with it, drawing his eyes to her fingers, then down the chain to her breasts. The gold and her skin and the black of her sweater, her hair, her kitchen, she knew all these things added up to something for him. She would work hard. She would stay on track.

He said, "You called me and I came."

"Oh, Lou." She paused in the house's quiet. She inhaled, resolved. "Thank you for coming."

She let him drive. It took a few kilometres for him to figure out the sticky clutch and the wobbly steering; the whole truck rattled more than it revved. She directed him onto the highway and they headed east.

"What are we going to listen to?" he asked her.

She made a sly face and held up a tape.

"Jesus, a tape? Doesn't this thing have a cd player?"

"Do you see a CD player? This tape will send you back in time."

"Lay it on me," he said and she slipped the tape in. The little black gate clunked shut behind it and over the sound of the truck on the highway, they heard the familiar hiss, the eight ascending notes, then the tinny opening synthesizer of EMF's "Unbelievable." He laughed.

"It's your tape! You made it for me. Remember?"

He turned up the volume. The town slipped from view and trees stretched out along either side of the highway, broken only by farms and driveways, the occasional field of stubble or turned dirt. They watched the scenery pass and the mixtape was a soundtrack fraught with other emotions from other times; fond memories were replaced by heartache and anxiety with the changing of the songs. Ramona co-piloted by pointing out which signs to pay attention to and which way to turn.

"Do you remember making this one? I was always saying write me a letter but you'd only ever put music on tapes and send it to me."

She tried to keep her eyes off him. It wasn't easy—she still felt thirteen about him. When she did glance over, she saw his sideburns were too long and flecked with gray. He needed a haircut. She remembered the time he'd sent her one of his dreadlocks in the mail—the rancid, fleshy smell of it.

"Remember, Lou? How you never wrote letters?" She smiled at him, at his hair blowing all over his face, at his worn shirt, his scuffed basketball shoes. "I wrote you so many letters."

"Should I say sorry?"

"I don't know. Never mind." She stared out the window. "I just thought it'd be different."

"What?"

"Everything." She watched the plateau give way to foothills as they got closer to the mountains. The rivers had shifted from wide, muddy brown to clear, quick creeks full of boulders. She felt far from her everyday life, but it also seemed like she'd been borrowing that life for a long time. Since before Charlie died. Since Louie. "I thought we'd be together by now." She peeked to see how he'd take that.

He squinted ahead. He cleared his throat. The song changed and he groaned suddenly and slapped the steering wheel. "Listen to that! Mo! I haven't heard that song since 1998."

They were almost in the Rockies proper. The tape finished and neither of them put in another one. They listened to the Suburban rattle in the wind the semi-trucks made as they passed and the day wore on, bright and beautiful. Ramona watched the trees pass in a blur, the green smear broken only by sudden deep ravines or creeks, and if she were in a different mood, she would have exclaimed over every body of turquoise water, told him again about travelling here with her parents when she was small, how her dad would stop every time she asked him to so she could swim or make dandelion chains. But her mouth was dry. Her mind was restless and she couldn't still it.

Louie stared ahead at the road. She propped her bare feet on the dashboard to see if he'd notice her ankles. She tried to remember she hadn't made her move yet—nothing was a given—but it was hard. The heat of their bodies filled the cab. The tape came to the end, flipped, and started side one again.

Her eyes ached. They'd been driving for hours. Louie

rubbed his face. There was a rest stop ahead with outhouses and picnic tables. He put his indicator on.

"Are you stopping? Wait, don't stop. There's a better place up ahead."

"What's wrong with this one?"

"Nothing, it's just the next one is better."

"I'm tired, Mo, and I want a drink."

She pulled a water bottle out of her satchel, cracked the lid, and held it out to him. "Please don't stop yet. The next rest stop is the place I want to do it."

"At a rest stop? I thought we were going to hike up a mountain."

She sighed and turned away. "We are, just after. The next rest stop is on the river and that's where I want to do it."

Louie flicked his indicator off and drank from the water bottle.

In her purse, besides the water bottle and a jar of almonds and raisins, a book, a notebook, her cell phone and a photo book of her and Louie, Ramona had a sealed urn full of Charlie's ashes. It wasn't what he'd wanted, but when the time came to deal with his body, it was all she could think of. She'd chosen an awful urn, too—white with blue stripes—like a vase from a Greek restaurant.

Charlie had died at the clinic. It was March, late at night after a calving call. He was catching up on the day's operations after hours, after all his scheduled appointments and operations had been bumped by farm calls. Ramona found him in the morning—he hadn't come to bed. His truck still in the driveway.

He'd always joked that he wanted to die with the dogs at his clinic. He told her that when he died she would have to haul him out back and put him in the incinerator with all the animals he'd put to sleep. He was going to knot the last stitch in a cat's abdomen after a spay, wash his hands, lie down on the floor, and die. She would have to clean up after him one way or another.

Ramona would hit Charlie's arm and tell him to stop it. He would pull her close and kiss her head. She'd never have been able to move him anywhere—he weighed two hundred and eighty pounds when he died. He was enormous. He always teased her.

He'd died at work, just like he'd wanted to, but it was years too soon. That part wasn't according to his plan. None of this was according to her plan—they had plane tickets to Arizona for spring break. And there were still too many things for Charlie to do, including rebuilding the fence and losing fifty pounds.

She had him cremated and bought an urn and brought it home after the funeral, along with the overabundance of flower arrangements. Then she went into the bedroom and pulled the curtains. It was a twilit time. The school hired a replacement teacher for her position. The mailbox filled with condolence cards and letters describing how Dr. Dearly had made such a difference in the lives of farmers and animals all across the valley. Flowers kept arriving. An article in the paper reported the accomplishments of the local vet who'd died too young, survived by his beloved wife—the town would miss their philanthropy, his hearty laugh—especially at the annual Rotary Club dinner and dance at the local Elk's Hall.

The plane tickets to Arizona expired and her Visa was charged for the hotel room they didn't stay in. Ramona kept the tourist sites bookmarked on her computer and she scrolled through them every now and then when she should have been dealing with the top of Charlie's dresser, which was still strewn with change and the leavings from his pockets: napkins with barns sketched out on them, toys from Christmas crackers, a photo of her from when she was twenty-three, an ampule of some sort of drug. She looked at her bookmarked sites and googled Louie's band. She pored over photos of Louie, his clothes and face black and pink from the stage lights; photos where his hair was long again. She noticed he had a scar the size of a thumbprint on his right cheekbone. She saw his arm around someone she didn't know—there were three photos of him with a dark-haired woman. She lay on her bed and caught up on Louie's career, his life without her. She kinked her back. Charlie's side of the bed drooped, and that irritated Ramona—the bed was wrecked because of him.

She started at the school again in September. There were children to teach. She had to make money. She did her best. She didn't, however, deal with Charlie's ashes. Instead, she called Louie. "Where are you?"

"A gig. Where are you?" It was tense. They hadn't spoken in years.

He asked if everything was okay and she couldn't get any words out. There was a long silence during which too many scenarios flitted through her head, until she blurted out that she needed him.

"What does that mean?" He swore, but he stayed on the phone. "You have to be more specific than that. I'm in St. Louis, Mona. I'm at work."

She thought fast. "I need a driver. To help me spread Charlie's ashes. This spring." A plan was coming together. She could almost see it whole: Louie would come to be with her. There'd been other times she'd called him to come and then cancelled on him—one time he'd even bought a plane ticket—but that was when she and Charlie had been fighting, when being just Mrs. Dearly—the vet's wife—didn't suit her, when her old plans for her life surged from the shadows and overtook her imagination. She'd faked Louie out too many times and he was right to be wary. He'd come, though. Who could say no to a widow?

In Charlie's Suburban, Louie put the indicator on and turned right off the highway. This rest stop was definitely nicer than the last: a stand of trees blocked the noise of the highway, and a small road led down to the parking lot, which was bordered by a river boisterous and green with silt. Signs leading to a trailhead stood next to the public washrooms. Louie parked the truck under the shade of a huge spruce.

"I'm going to the bathroom," he said.

Ramona sat for a second in the heat of the ticking truck after he'd left, then got out and walked down to the river. A kingfisher sat in a branch overhanging the opposite bank. She crouched to watch and see if it would dive. An eddy swirled under the branch and the kingfisher's attention was underwater. She heard a truck gearing down on the highway and for a moment the day seemed to stretch and pause, pinning her in the heat on the river bank, holding her against the earth. While her attention was diverted the bird dove. Just as quickly it launched upward again, a veil of water drops falling into the river behind it, a tiny minnow in its beak. It flickered through the air further down the river. She sat down on the bank, then lay back and let the sun soak into her skin. She closed her eyes.

When she opened them Louie was sitting beside her. He had the small cooler she'd packed, out of which he pulled a bag of sliced salami. She sat up. He pulled out crusty buns and two pears and set them beside her on the bank. It was so familiar for them to be having a picnic. It thrilled her.

Wasps came, interested in the pears and the smell of meat. She put it back in the cooler and flipped the lid shut.

"Here." She handed Louie his sandwich. Wasps zipped around their faces, inspecting the crumbs on their clothes and the crusts of bun that fell to the rocks.

They ate watching the water. The wasps congregated on the cooler lid, searching for a way in. The kingfisher came back for seconds. Another kingfisher joined it on its branch over the water. She thought about telling Louie how she was barely managing, how she needed him there day to day, but she didn't—she'd never be able to say how she felt. It was like writing letters to him had sapped any ability to really talk about things. They'd had more misunderstandings and fights due to talking than she cared to think about. Her wedding came to mind, how he'd stormed out. She'd said the wrong thing. Then there were the things he hadn't said as a teenager, or as a man, or as a friend—she could feel the words hovering around them. Talking wasn't the answer.

"I'm going to get some water." He stood and walked back to the truck. He came back with her water bottle and his guitar. He took a drink, offered it to her, then sat down to tune.

"Play 'Me and Bobby McGee', Louie. Please?" She touched his arm. "Remember how you thought it was about two men? That was so funny."

"I still like it better that way. Platonic."

"Hm." She felt a flash of irritation that he thought differently than she did. "I like it as a love song."

He strummed out the first chords and started singing. He sang the first verse and she joined in on the chorus, just softly, and it killed her how sweet their voices sounded together, and she wondered if he was right about the song: it still worked if it was about friendship, loss, hitchhiking, what got left behind. She lay on the bank and thought about it. Eventually clouds formed and it got cooler. They packed up the lunch and Louie's guitar and stood by the truck.

"Well?"

"Right. We'll need my purse."

"Where are we going?"

"Just up the trail to the falls. It won't take more than an hour."

They walked and she took his hand in hers. Her palm sweat against his. The dappling of the sun through the trees made the forest seem darker; ahead, fewer rods of light broke through the forest canopy. They walked and their footfalls cast up brief explosions of dust.

The summer they were twelve, before Louie left, they'd tried to build a fort in the field behind her house. They deepened a hollow under a haphazard stack of downed, limbed trees that they thought they could live in. They hauled a mattress they'd found in a ditch across the field, flattening the tall grass, getting it stuck on prickle bushes and stumps, swearing and laughing at the swear words they made up: crack-asser! Dumbdefuck! They laughed like there was never anything funnier.

They'd taken a break mid-field to catch their breath, and flopped down onto the mattress. The tall grasses waved over them, gold and rasping. It was mid-summer and nothing had gone wrong yet. The sky above them was clear of clouds, the edges of it more white than blue, the promise of what lay ahead of them so enormous it felt balanced on their foreheads.

The hilarity wore off and they breathed quietly beside one another—Ramona still a girl in every sense of the word: childish body, desires so simple they could be drawn with chalk and still made sense of. Louie's teeth were still shifting around in his jaw and he would look different in half a year as his face matured and his body sturdied up. He would lose his snub nose and his high eyebrows and gain an air of forced cool, like nothing could surprise him. He would grow six inches in two years, straining all the connections in his body until they lengthened and then his boyhood would be gone so completely it would take a parent, or Ramona, to remember back to the boy he'd been.

Ramona felt she was breathing in the essence of the wild roses—she could imagine pink flowers ghosting up her nostrils and their freshness infusing her body. She'd looked over at Louie and he'd looked at her and for a long moment neither of them moved.

They were walking up the trail, him with a backpack, her with her purse. It was hot. She followed him, eyes on his feet, then his hips, then she was remembering the smell of him, the cinnamon and hot-sunlight smell of the spot behind his ear, under his hair. She stopped.

"Louie, listen."

He stopped and turned to her. Around them insects hummed and a bird sang two dull notes and a third.

"What?"

She stood, her throat tight. "I mean, what if you just stayed with me? Like forever. Like," she swallowed. "Like it was always going to be." She'd said it. Sweat dripped down her spine.

Louie drew his brows together. He shook his head slightly and she rushed to stop him.

"I mean, we could move if you don't want to live where Charlie and I lived, but we'd be together. We could buy a house." Her voice sounded not like her own, but high and anxious.

"Mo, listen."

She put her hand up, palm out. "I'd move anywhere you wanted. I could come on tour. I could be your assistant. I'm good at organizing things. I know a lot about travel bookings and logistics."

He stopped her. "Mona, no. I met someone."

She already knew that. Did she already know that? It wasn't

49

his fault. The food she'd eaten roiled under her diaphragm. She thought she might throw up. "Why didn't you tell me?"

"I did. I wrote you a letter. I told you about Jill in the letter. I sent a CD, too. The new album. Didn't you get it?"

It was slipping away. She could feel it slipping. Ramona remembered the mattress they'd killed themselves dragging across the field. They never managed to get it into the fort. It stayed in the field and after they'd gone Ramona imagined it white and rimmed with wild flowers, but she once went back to find it during a university break and was disgusted by the mouldering, broken-down thing exactly where they'd left it.

She pushed him in the centre of his chest, not hard. "No, I didn't get a letter. Maybe you didn't send it. I would have got it if you sent it. Where did you send it? Did you send it to my address?"

"Of course I did."

"Well, where is it?" She was mad. She'd started to yell, one arm gripping her purse, the other scrabbling inside it for something to help, to make things better. Sweat drooled down her back into her shorts. "Where is it if you sent it? Did you get my letters?"

"Which ones? Did you send some?"

"I sent one last week! Louie, I sent a letter last week! Oh my God, our letters aren't getting through!"

She stopped scrabbling. She could hear the roar of the water. It sounded like Louie's breathing on her cassette tapes, his mouth so close to the microphone it deafened her. She could see his chest in his loose shirt rise and fall. Her heart thumped hard. She couldn't hear his thoughts. That's what was wrong. She knew him well enough, but she didn't know his thoughts. She didn't know anything.

"I was sending them to New Orleans. Your apartment in New Orleans."

"Ramona, I moved in with Jill. I haven't had that address for a year."

She could hear wasps. "Did you have your mail forwarded?" Her words came slow. She wanted to know about the mail forwarding, but it wasn't what she needed to know. What if she'd missed it? Not the letters, but all of it. "What about your letters to me? Why didn't I get them?"

"Hey, listen. Mo. Take a breath. I know this is hard. Why don't you tell me three things? Not what you're afraid of. Three things you love. Remember that game?"

She shook her head, no. She was shaking. She wasn't going to play that game. But she could see Charlie in his X-ray darkroom wearing the lead vest, grinning at her, holding up some picture of a dog leg with a pin in it. He was proud of the pin. He'd wanted to show her. She'd come over to see why he was late for supper.

She saw Charlie in the driver's seat shouting at her over the sound of the wind, the windows all down. He was laughing.

She saw him with his reading glasses on in front of the computer, his chin resting on his hand, his leg jigging up and down, his hand in the fur of a dog he'd brought in from the clinic who was too sick to be left alone. She was bringing him a whisky.

"Mo?" Louie reached a hand toward her.

"No, I can't. I don't want to play. I've got to go."

But she didn't have to go. The smell of hot pine needles wafted from the duff at the edges of the path. She could smell the dirt underfoot. She heard the rush of the river, her shadow a puddle at her feet. Where could she go from here? She needed to find the letters, hers most especially. All her thoughts were in them. She had no thoughts, maybe she had nothing at all, if she didn't have her letters.

Her fingers closed around her keys and she let her purse drop to the dust. She didn't stop to retrieve it. She turned and sprinted down the path, her hair flying out behind her. She ran through bushes, pushing aside branches, away from the river, back toward Charlie's truck, her lungs heaving. Sun and then shade and then blinding sun again, she ran so fast, her feet pounding on the packed dirt trail, her breath ripping in and out of her throat. She felt like she could go on forever. She could hear a faint voice in her head, a voice growing louder, words in time with the thump of her feet. It was her voice, clear and rising. She ran on.

BARE LIMBS IN SUMMER HEAT

"Dustin, where are we going?" A strip of light on the horizon was all that was left of sunset, three thirty in the afternoon, Christmas Eve. For a long time neither of us had spoken over the tires' hum. I looked out the windshield over the winter fields and could feel the length of the highway stretching out behind us all the way to Prince Rupert and the Pacific. Ahead the asphalt was black and bare. Thin wisps of snow scudded across the road in the wake of semi-truck trailers. I rolled my head on the headrest and stared at my brother, waiting for his response.

"Weins'. Not Brian from high school, Brian's dad's. Weins, the elder."

I rolled my eyes. "Why do you need me again?"

"It could get messy. Caesarean, I bet. I might need your help."

"But of everyone in the house, I'm the smallest. Joe could help, or the boys, they're almost as big as you are now."

"Yeah, but they were busy playing cards. Joe should be with his kids."

"And I shouldn't?" On fire immediately, heat spreading over my body, I rose to it. Like always. He did that to me.

"Not what I meant. Aside from Shelley, you're the one who might actually know how to help. And Shelley's pregnant."

I snorted. Dustin couldn't let anyone forget. His thing lately was child-rearing books. I was still fuming over the ones he'd recommended to me—*Raising the Moral Child, Parenting with Heart For Happiness*—did he think I didn't know what I was doing? My children were teenagers, for Christ's sake. I took it personally, as I did with anything he suggested.

"It's been years since I helped on a call. I don't know if I remember how a Caesarean goes."

"Well, let me tell you."

And he proceeded to tell me, at length, while I ignored him. I remembered enough about calving calls to know how gross and boring they could be. I wanted to stare out the window, but frost had choked off all but a small black circle of dark. I love frost filigrees. I remembered following them with my finger as a kid, horrified and fascinated I could wreck it just by being near, leaving a line of melt in my wake, a thin black path of clear window behind me. "Why are they calving this time of year?" I forgot I was trying to ignore him.

He shrugged. "It's early." It sounded like there would be more. I waited for it. There was: "But maybe there's no right time to have kids."

"God, Dustin."

He smiled at his rare joke, pleased with himself, and I watched the night whiz past the windshield, cold and bleak.

The headlights cast a weak glow that barely lit the trees on either side of the highway. "What's wrong with your lights?" I shifted around, knocking crumpled coffee cups and takeout bags with my boots. I peered into the backseat at the silver calf-puller, the buckets and ropes, the dust of hundreds of calls ground into the upholstery. "Jesus. It's filthy in here."

"No dirtier than when Dad had it."

"If it was good enough for Dad?" I shook my head. I considered not getting into it, but it was so easy. "Gonna keep it all the same forever? Gonna keep driving this thing until it falls to pieces, till your bumper falls off in some barnyard, till your muffler lands behind you on the highway, or the engine dies and you're stuck in a snowstorm and someone finds your bones in springtime, dead and stupid, and just the same as Dad, driving his old truck, running his old practice, living in the same house we grew up in? Good for you, Dustin. Don't aim too high. It's not worth it."

He said nothing. I watched his jaw clench while I goaded him, but he kept his hands at ten and two, kept his tires between the white lines. I kept at him until he barked back. "Shut up, Celia! God."

I was heating up again. Sweat trickled down from my armpits and my heart banged hard for a few beats more, then slowed in the car's silence. It was an old argument. One we'd had a million times since Mom and Dad sold him the practice for a pittance. I didn't even care—I wasn't a vet, and didn't want to be, so I didn't need it, the house or the practice. Joe and I had plenty, but it smarted all the same. In my opinion, if you have two kids, you split your assets down the middle. I would've sold Dustin my half. It would have worked out the same, but without the sharp spike in my chest each time I thought of it. My blood pressure started rising again. "It's just lazy, Dustin." I turned to look at him in the glow of the instrument panel. "What happened to you? You're so complacent. You only care about work and Shelley and fucking moral child-rearing." I could picture the stupid cover of the book. "You used to be..." I searched for the word, "Fun. At least. We used to have fun, Dusty. Didn't we?"

He was quiet. Deciding whether or not to let my words die down or to get back into it with me. He tilted his head side to side, stretching his neck, then stared straight ahead again. "Yeah, we did."

He didn't say more. We both stared out at the dark road ahead of us, and I felt the loss of him all over again. I could sometimes will the old world of the two of us close for a second—our small bodies hurtling around the farmyard, blasting from this imagined place to that, swinging from the pussy willow tree, jumping off the chicken house roof—

but not often. Sometimes, when my boys were small, I'd mistake their thin four-year-old or six-year-old arms for his, Dustin's little brown hands and scrawny arms reaching up for me to give him a boost into a tree or trying to catch me as I kept just out of reach. I'd called each of them Dusty accidentally at least once, and the boys laughed, but it was always a double-take for me. I was startled not to be six to his four, eight to his six, surprised to be without him, to be forty-four and a mother of twin teenage boys. I was so far from my brother in every aspect of adult life.

I stared at the night beyond the windshield, feeling stupid. It wasn't like I'd lost him—here he was, after all. Here we both were, together at Christmas, like any siblings might be. Of course, we weren't inseparable anymore. Of course, we'd grown up and away and into our own lives. I let my head rest on the cold, frosty window, the hair on my temple sticking to it, soaking up the melt. I inhaled the stuffy, straw-smelling air. My shoulders dropped.

"I'm sorry. I'm a little wound up." I watched my breath sigh out a white cloud. We were quiet a while. My head was cold against the window, and my body grew cold too as my sweat—and my temper—cooled. I rubbed my hands together and chanced saying something about it. "Does the heater not work?"

"It never did."

"Never?" I thought about that. It seemed true. I remembered falling asleep in my snowsuit in the back, that sweet feeling of puffy cushion all around me, the cold air on my cheeks and nose. "You're right. The windows were always frosty. I remember making tongue prints on the glass. Dad would yell."

We laughed remembering our bum-shaped tongue prints all over the inside of the windows. It was something.

I could see two red reflectors on a post glinting in the headlights. Dustin put on his blinker. We followed the ruts in the snow down a winding driveway toward a house. He turned from that main drive onto a fainter set of ruts that ran off to the right. We drove up to a two-storey pole barn that even at night, silhouetted against the glow from town, looked old, likely drafty and full of mice. Light leaked out of the barn through cracks between the boards. He parked. I pulled Dad's old duffle coat around me. It was so big it hung to my shins. Under the coat my sparkly silver sweater prickled and I thought about how my tight black pants were ill-suited to barn work. But so was I.

I sat in the car a moment longer and listened to the engine tick. I heard Dustin haul open the door and start banging around in the back. I waited, then I pulled open the passenger door and got out. The wind took my breath. I hugged myself tight, tucking my face into the coat's shearling collar, and tramped around the vehicle through the deep snow. Around the back I watched Dustin grab a bucket and two jugs of still-warm water—they'd been piping hot when we left the house. He held them out to me. I took them and let them hang heavy at the end of my arms like bell gongs, the bucket strung awkwardly on its metal handle over my wrist and sticking out from my body like a stiff silver flag. He hefted his case in one hand and the calf puller in the other and set off in the snow for the barn. I followed behind, swimming in his old gumboots, which I clomped down into the larger prints his new boots made.

It wasn't usual for me to follow, but it felt right given we were at work now, his work, and he had a role to play. I wasn't sure of my role yet, but I'd played assistant before, with Dad, and I knew how to do that. There were rules around being at Dad's work when we were kids: no talking unless it was an emergency; no fooling around or you'd be sent back to the truck; no asking questions until it was all over, and then only if it was a happy outcome. If not, no one felt like talking.

Inside, the barn was lit with a bare bulb screwed into an extension cord, strung over the rafters to illuminate a wide aisle flanked by dark stalls. The light left deep shadows on all it didn't touch and the hay was old and trampled, dirty with manure and use. A cow lay heaving in the centre of the aisle, tied by a halter to a beam. Her neck stretched awkwardly toward the wall. Her wet, shallow breathing was the only noise in the barn. I stopped when I saw her. Nausea washed through my guts. I set the bucket and jugs down, stepped into the shadows and turned away.

A farmer walked toward us from the other end of the barn. "Hey Doc," he said. "And hello, there," he called to me. "Glad you could make it. Sorry about the bad timing."

"Don't worry about it, Glen. Can't be helped. Now, how's she doing?"

"Maybe you can tell me. She's been breathing like that for hours. We got her tied up there and we tried to figure out what that calf's doing, but we can't tell. I reached in and felt something. A nose, I think. Feels big, anyway."

Dustin set his case down by the wall and walked toward the cow. The blue collar of his vest stuck up from inside his dust-coloured coverall. I watched him lay his hand on the cow's flank and run it up her side, and I heard him start, low and mumbling, to talk to the cow, just like we'd always heard Dad do it. "There's a girl. That's right, it's just me. There we go, there we go. Not so bad, is it? Not so bad."

I'd seen it calm cows before, a million times I'd seen it and heard it, but I'd never noticed its effect on me. I felt my chest unclench. I fought to keep in mind it was Dustin and not Dad talking, and the talking shouldn't work because

Dustin was Dustin, but it worked, and I calmed. I felt my breathing slow and my hands relax.

The cow, who had calmed as well, suddenly flinched and breathed harder, a contraction bunching up her hind end in spasm toward her front. Her eyes rolled white in her head. Her legs stuck straight out stiff and then sagged, her breath rasping. Dustin's hand was still on her stomach. "She been labouring long?"

"A few hours, like I said. She lay down about an hour ago." The farmer stepped forward into the light with Dustin. The cow relaxed against the halter and blinked and breathed. The farmer put his hand on her neck where it bent funny and stroked the red fur.

"This is her first time, right?" Dustin had his stethoscope out and listened to the cow's distended abdomen, then placed it on her back, listening to her heart.

"That's right. She's a good-natured sort, but she's having a tough time with it."

"She's pretty small."

I watched the men's hands on the cow and the cow resting between contractions. I knew the smooth, warm plastic of the stethoscope and the cool of its flat face from being allowed to hold it while Dad worked. It could have been a new one—it could have been Dustin's stethoscope from vet school—but it looked like Dad's. I knew how the stubby plugs felt in Dustin's ears because I'd felt them before, straining to hear over my own breathing, trying to keep my brother still while I sat on him, squashing him down to listen to his little beating bird heart when we were kids. I stood behind a stall wall and looked into the bright aisle. The wind blew between the cracks in the walls of the barn behind me. I pressed myself up against the wood and watched the heifer bunch and seize again, the contraction pulling her muscles taut. I saw my brother's hands stroke the fur on the cow's broad forehead. I saw the blank whites of her eyes.

"You didn't feel any feet, did you, Glen?"

"Nope, just a big old nose. You want me to help you get her up?"

"If you don't mind."

"Come on, girl, up you get." He whacked the heifer on the back near her tail. She startled, but didn't rise. "Come on, now." He grabbed her tail and bent it in half and whacked the cow again. She startled and lowed and struggled to get her legs under her. Dustin got his arms beneath her back and he and the farmer heaved her up. She stood splay-legged and wobbly under the light, the halter holding her head down, now at a different angle. The farmer patted her and came close against her side, there if she started to fall.

"Thanks. Now let's see what we can do." Dustin walked over to his bucket and jugs of water where I'd dropped them at the barn entrance. He slopped enough water into the bucket to wash his hands and arms, then he picked up his brush and bucket and took them back to the cow. He scooped water on her vulva and washed it with his hand. He tried to lighten the mood. "There must be divine logic in the placement of the arsehole over the vagina, but I can't figure it."

I winced. We weren't religious, but ninety-five percent of the town of McCall were. Was it risky for him to say that? I watched the farmer's face, but he only smiled. We watched Dustin scrub the cow and walk away dripping from elbow to fingertip.

He looked like Dad in this light, or this circumstance. Maybe it was his gait. He was broader in the shoulders, shorter, so he didn't stoop as much as Dad, but his forehead was the same, and the way he pushed his glasses up his nose. Even his hair—short on the sides, the little bit left on top combed over to the right—just like Dad's.

Dustin opened his black case and stepped out the trays that accordioned from the box. He squirted lubricant all over his right hand and arm, then walked to the cow's hind end. "The lubricant will help her clean any poop out of there. It'll help me get in and the calf get out without hurting her." He said this to himself as much as to the farmer, I knew. I recognized Dad's teaching voice—low and slow, and a little apologetic. He turned his attention back to the cow. "There's a girl, that's right, don't worry about me." He slid his hand into the swollen vulva, pushing as far into the vaginal canal as he could. He made a face. "You sure you felt a nose, there?"

The cow had blinked when he slid his arm in, then she strained against him. He winced and stood still as she contracted on the calf and his arm. He pushed farther into her. "Relax, girl, relax." The cow's breathing was loud and she lowed as Dustin probed her insides.

The barn creaked and moaned in the wind. I knew this part of the farm call well: the figuring and finding out, the examination and questions, but I also recognized the audacity—if that was the word—of the men. I'd always felt the cow's part, the indignity of needing help, and I knew the potential for everything to go wrong in an instant, so the necessity of the intervention, but I also recognized the matter-of-fact invasion of the cow's body. Like growing up a girl. Maybe that was what I meant by audacity—maybe I meant passivity when forced face-to-face with science, the lie-back-and-let-it-happen of the Pap-smear or the breast exam. It was complicated. There was the cow, the pregnancy, the misfortune of a too-big calf or a placenta previa, or prolapse, or whatever, and then there was the way doctors solved those problems.

Dad had gone into these nights with gentleness, and Dustin did, too, but the boldness of their interference was something I couldn't get over. My own Caesarean was ever-present, even though it happened ages ago. The way my body lurched from side to side behind the blue curtain, hiding my open abdomen from me, what I'd felt despite the epidural, when they'd hauled Jonas, and then Sean, out of me. I was helpless—insensate, but also helpless to the events—and in order to survive I'd had to submit to such gross and base proceedings. I leaned against the rough boards of the enclosure and sweated in my coat, the backs of my legs freezing.

Dustin slid his arm out of the cow, bringing forth a gush of red fluid that splattered over his boots onto the hay. The barn shifted in the wind gusts and snow drifted in across the floor.

"I don't know, Glen. I think that's the cervix, not a nose. I hate to say it, but I think she's got a twisted uterus."

The farmer paled. "Shit, doc. That doesn't sound good."

Dustin shook his head. "Not good, but maybe not totally bad. If it's a partial twist I might be able to get in there and lift the calf to untwist it. It's a tough go. I'll have to figure out which way she's twisted and lift the calf, which isn't easy, but it might turn out okay. Thing is, if it's a full twist you might be looking at butchering her."

"Oh, we'll be shipping her for sure after this. Can't calve, can't keep her."

"True. But listen, if it's a full twist, we've only got a tiny hope of a live cow, live calf situation. And I couldn't even get in there far enough to tell if the calf's still alive." He stood with his wet arm hanging at his side, but I saw the tension in his jaw.

The farmer rubbed his face with one hand, smoothing out his whiskers, then roughing them up. He flapped his arms. "Christ, I don't know."

"Look, what we'll do is I'll give it a try untwisting it from the back. If that doesn't work, I'll go in from the side. I had a call out to Jones's the other week just the same that worked out beautifully. But I have to tell you, I always mention butchering when we've got uterine torsion. If you know you'll be shipping her, the Caesarean'll give you the best chance for a live calf and a salvageable cow—but if she gets stressed or shocky, it won't end well. It's a big calf, for sure, and she's small, Glen. We're in for a time here."

The farmer took his toque off and scrubbed his head with it, then put it back on. I could see the nape of his neck wet with sweat and I felt for him. It would be an expensive night with no guarantees.

"Got it, Doc," he said, and nodded hard once. "We figured it'd be bad, but we didn't know how bad. That's why we called."

"I'm the last resort, that's for sure." They both laughed, but nervously.

I wasn't hearing the cow moan, and then suddenly, that's all I could hear—with each breath, her voice droned like a far-off fog horn in the night, sorrowful and relentless. Saliva drooled from her mouth. I watched my brother walk back to the bucket to wash his hands and arms again. Steam rose from his skin in the cold air. I thought about how much washing was truly necessary and how much was punctuation in the play Dustin was performing, but that wasn't right or fair; I looked at the dirty, shitty hay and the flakes of dust snowing down from the beams in the ceiling and was amazed again that any animal came out of surgery in a barn all right. I'd almost died, and I'd delivered in a room that smelled of disinfectant.

Dustin lubed up his arm and pushed it into the cow again. I watched his face carefully, but I couldn't tell by his grimaces and creased brow what he felt. He was pushing hard, bracing his feet against the barn floor and straining to get further into the cow.

"If I can push past the cervix, I can try and lift the calf," he muttered through clenched teeth. He stepped back, softening his arm for a second, then pushed hard into her again. Then he stepped back again and swore. "No go, Glen. Caesarean, for sure. I'm sorry to say it."

He went back to his case and got ready for surgery. The farmer talked to Dustin about other farmers and he raised his voice over the cow's lowing when he had to. I walked away from the stall toward the wall of the barn. I found a good-sized hole between the boards and put my eye to it.

The moon had risen and the field was white, blank with snow. It looked like the start of a fairy tale. The black line of trees on the other side of the pasture made a rough-hewn horizon, jagged and saw-toothed in the moonlight, and the barnyard, lit as if in daylight, was desolate and empty. A path led down a low hill toward the house.

A dog sat on the path. He stared at the trees across the field and then quickly turned his head toward the house. A woman came out the door and stomped down the stairs, peering around a tray so she didn't slip. I saw the dog run up and hop around her, then follow her along the path to the barn. She held the tray firm despite the dog's excitement, and the Thermos and cups balanced on top stayed put. The wind blew snow across the yard and great silver wisps rose up toward the moon then drifted back to earth. It was a perfect short film. I felt warmer watching the world from inside four walls, even if they were drafty.

The barn door banged open and the farmer's wife bustled in with her tray aloft. "Rotten night, Doctor! A downright rotten night to be called out away from your own festivities."

"Not to worry. Just family at home. We kept it pretty quiet this year."

"Not for long, I hear."

"Alice," her husband chided.

Dustin looked at the woman closely, then said, "Oh right. My sister's here for Christmas. She's arrived already, actually." He nodded toward me in the shadows of the barn, but the woman ignored him.

"Oh no, Doctor, I meant your good news! A new baby! You be quiet, Glen, it's just congratulations. Any cause to celebrate, I'll take it. How's she doing?"

Dustin looked confused. "Shelley?"

"Oh, go on with you, I mean this poor dear." She set her tray down on a hay bale and walked up to the cow and started stroking her fur, scratching around her ears and forehead.

Dustin stood ready with a razor, a scalpel waiting in his coverall pocket, blade up. "Not too bad, Alice. She's a brave girl."

"She is. She's a good girl, one of our nicest and best be-haved, and now look at her. Knocked up out of turn and struggling to calve. I hope you can help her."

"I'll try. If you'll just step aside…"

Dustin moved in and started shaving a strip in the cow's side. Quickly, efficiently, his strokes bared her skin. In sec-onds he had a tidy rectangle just under her hip bone and toward her stomach. He pulled a syringe and a vial of freez-ing out of his pocket. He shook the vial, sucked the fluid into the syringe, then walked around to the cow's back end and picked her tail up, syringe held high in the other hand. He pumped the tail up and down twice, watching where it hinged, then he pushed the needle in above that and plunged the freezing into the cow. He froze the area he'd shaved also, then he waited for the freezing to take hold. I watched him rub the spot he'd poked—I'd seen this same procedure so many times. He had too. I wondered if he'd been bored in vet school, if he'd daydreamed while he went through motions he'd known from his boyhood of watching Dad. Did it feel different now that it was he who had to remember what to do? I shivered to imagine how I would handle this situation—the pressure would be awful. But here was my baby brother, smiling and joking with the family, about to cut open a cow to bare her insides to the winter.

"Here we go," he said, and he washed the bare skin on her side with iodine. He took up his scalpel and in two slices he made a six-inch opening. He cut another slice across the top to make a T. Then he put his scalpel down and slid his hand into the hole.

"Didn't think you'd made it big enough even for your hand, Doc. Don't know how you're going to get a calf out of there," said the farmer.

"Small incisions heal faster. There's less chance for infection. I can always make it bigger if I need to. And the hole the calf should have come out of isn't much bigger."

That got a chuckle from the couple. I rolled my eyes.

Dustin leaned in to the cow, his arm deep inside her. I imagined it snaking around, like he was walking arms out in the dark looking for someone, trying not to bump into the furniture. I couldn't believe he could do these things—it impressed me, but I'd never tell him so. How could I, when this was the boy who'd followed me around and done everything I'd told him to when we were small? He'd followed me all the way to university on the coast, into art school, but he'd dropped that fast when Dad got frail. Mom and Dad were delighted when he applied to vet school. He'd won Best Child Ever Forever and Always.

I'd asked him in the car if he remembered the stories Dad used to tell.

"Course I do," he'd said, and I felt like he meant I should stop talking, like I was an idiot to suggest anyone could forget something like that. And I did feel like an idiot for a moment, but only for a moment, and I'd barrelled ahead anyway.

"There was always a brother and a sister. There was a brother and a sister and an adventure. Peril. They'd almost die and then they'd use their smarts to save each other. One time they were swallowed by a snake, remember? They thought they were walking on a road, but it was the body of a gargantuan black snake who ate children, and it ate them. That surprised me. Like somehow I thought the kids were immune to being eaten by a child-eating snake. But it ate them and then they had to figure out how to get out of the snake. How to get home again. All the stories were about getting home again. Why do you think that was? Why would he tell us stories like that?" I'd turned to face him, shifting in my seat so he was my point of view.

"He was trying to stay awake." Dustin's eyes were on the road. He was explaining again. "He was always tired after a farm call." His face was a pale stone in the dashboard's glow.

I huffed. "It was more than that. They were crazy stories. Wild. Children in the wilderness. Hot air balloons. Kites that could carry cities. A brother and a sister and a wolf pack. Accordions. And we were always in the back. Remember? Why were we in the back? It was the seventies. We weren't wearing seatbelts, and if we weren't on the bench seat in the back, we were in the very back. Why didn't we sit in the front?"

"Because we fought about it."

"That's not why." I tried to remember. "We were jammed together between the seats. We held hands at the scary parts. Dad said settle down back there, and then he'd start the story. We'd say *go on, go on*."

"I remember that."

"Right? *Go on, Daddy, go on*."

Dustin pulled his arm out of the cow and again bloody fluid came out. He said, "I think I've got him," then he took his scalpel and sliced the hole a little longer. He came over to the bucket of warm water and washed his hands and arms again. As he turned back to the cow, it swayed against the farmer.

"Whoa, girl," Weins said, planting his feet and leaning against the cow. His wife came in to offer the pillar of her body. They held up the weight of the cow together. The sounds the woman made for the cow came out in a stream, a susurrus of comfort. I watched them working together and imagined them working that way all day every day, moving over their land, planting, harvesting, tending to the animals. I saw them glance at each other and then shift a bit, so they held the cow more evenly, then the farmer leaned down and with a fist, knocked the cow's stiff legs out to the sides to give her more of a solid base, like a sawhorse. When the cow's weight was off them, the wife stood near her husband and he put his arm around her. "Still okay, Doc?" he asked.

"Just fine." Dustin had both arms in the incision so deep his cheek rested on the red curls of the cow's fur. His eyes were closed.

I turned my attention back the farmer and his wife, easy with one another despite the desperation of the evening. They were a team. Our parents were not like that. I thought of them making Christmas dinner when we were small— Dad standing like a fencepost at the stove stirring the gravy while Mom careened around the kitchen like a trapped bird. Dad made the gravy. Mom did everything else. On Halloween, he did the pumpkin. Mom said carving pumpkins wasn't that different from surgery, but I couldn't remember a time I saw her watching one of Dad's surgeries. I didn't know how she'd know, except it was more convenient for her if he did that work so she could roast the meat or open the wine. I could still hear Mom's commentary unbidden. I could still see Dad sigh and reach for his drink.

I watched Dustin shift around so he had one foot under the cow and one leg out, slightly behind him, like he was on the starting line of a race. His face was peaceful except for the furrow between his brows. "Just a minute, now. Just a minute and…okay, here we go." He bent deep in his knees and hauled, pressing into the cow's side, straining to lift the dead weight of the calf. He straightened his legs, lifting as hard as he could, his face a skeleton's grimace, teeth bared, all the veins standing out on his forehead and neck. Like a cross between He-Man and Skeletor, I thought, and was pleased to think he might enjoy the comparison to his childhood hero and antihero, but the feeling fell out of me as I watched him struggle. Everything he had he put into this effort to shift the calf and loosen the twist. He shuffled his feet closer together and pulled again. A groan came from him that rivaled the cow's moans. The farmer and his wife leaned toward him, ready to help but unable to offer anything to the fight going on inside the body of the cow.

"I can't," Dustin said, stepping back and drawing his arms out. He was breathing hard. "I can't get it on my own." His bare arms dripped pink onto the straw. "I maybe got the twist out—I know I pushed the other stuff out of the way, and I got him lifted up a bit, but we'll have to wait and see if I got things sorted. I'm going to need help with this next part. Glen, I'll see if I can grab his legs now. You pull my waist, okay?"

The farmer walked over and wrapped his arms around Dustin's waist. Dustin went back into his runner's crouch and reached inside the cow.

The farmer matched his stance to Dustin's. "I'm ready."

"Okay. On three. One, two, three."

They leaned back and pulled. Nothing happened.

"Okay, one more time. Pull." The cow swayed toward them, but the calf didn't budge. "Damn it."

The farmer let go of his waist.

Dustin looked around him at the calf puller leaned up against the fence, and shook his head. "I don't want to crank it out. I've seen too many calves mangled by the puller. We need muscles." He looked at the farmer's wife, a tiny woman, tough, but not strong.

"Our son Brian's at his in-law's house for the holidays. It's just down the way. I'll run on up to the house and give him a call."

"Well, Alice, there might not be enough time," Dustin said.

"What else is there to do? I want to help. I may not be a muscle-man, but I'm quick! I'll just run up and get on the phone. It won't take no time at all." She was out the door in a second.

Dustin turned to speak to the farmer again, but then stopped. He turned around and peered into the gloom. I froze. "Sis? Looks like I need you after all."

It turned me into a child to be asked to help—I wanted to run away. I was sixteen the last time I helped Dad on a farm call. I'd stood in my new jeans holding a prolapsed uterus while the farmer's son, a starting forward from my high school basketball team, looked on. Dad washed the huge bag of muscle hanging out of the cow's vagina, talking on and on, intent on the job, intent on his task, oblivious to me standing there sweating, arms shaking from the sheer weight of the uterus—a watermelon-sized, half-full garbage bag of hot, living flesh. I should have been amazed, holding a live organ like that, or I should have felt nonchalant, having helped out so many times before, but instead I was furious. I knew from that moment on my social chances at school were shot. Even if that boy was a farm kid who knew about all the weird shit that happened when things went wrong with livestock, it mattered that he saw me holding a uterus while my dad washed it. It mattered that I'd seen his family vulnerable to the cost of the call, that I'd seen the inside of his barn, and it mattered to me that my new jeans had been bled on and covered in shit—even fresh out of the wash I wouldn't wear them to school again. It would have been different if it'd been Dustin helping out that night. There'd be some cachet in it; he'd be a hero. I didn't know how, or why, but I knew it was different for a girl. Vet school was out of the question for me. It got a laugh out of farmers, how emphatically I'd shake my head when they asked if I would grow up to follow in Dad's footsteps.

Dustin grinned at me, indicating my fancy black pants, and said, "Should have put on a coverall, hey? Oh well, it's probably a treat for the cow to see you done up so nice just to help her deliver."

"Shut up, Dustin."

The farmer kept his mouth shut, but it wobbled at the edges.

"So, I'll grab the calf. Celia, you grab me around the waist. Glen, if you don't mind, you grab Celia around her waist, and we'll all pull on three."

The farmer whacked his hands together and then brushed them on his pants. "I guess it'll be if you don't mind, won't it?"

"I don't mind." I came up behind my brother and slid my arms around his waist. It was shocking to feel his solid body. I blushed at the intimate contact, bewildered by the fact of grown-up him, and surprised by my shyness—we'd bathed together a million times as kids. We'd peed off a million high things just to see the piss splash down and enjoy the sun on our naked bits. It'd just been so long since I'd touched him in any way other than a stiff hug hello or an equally awkward goodbye.

He needed my help. This was the only forum in our lives he'd ever ask for it. He was the steady one, the stable kid with reasonable grades and commitments to basketball and volleyball. I was the wild card—an A in math one semester and then failing the next. I was a star for three years running track then quit in my final year and gave no reason. If someone had asked—and I guess I'd wanted Dustin to ask—I might've said how scared I was to really try. What if I tried and wasn't good enough? Instead, I could be counted on not to be counted on, while Dustin was solid. He was my best friend as a child, my opposite as a teenager, and my enemy the moment he dropped me to run home to our parents. Dramatic, but that was my role in the family. His was to fulfill our parents' expectations.

I'd tried to punish him by removing myself from his life but he was so busy with school he didn't notice. And then he'd met Shelley. I secretly liked Shelley better than any woman I'd ever met, but I pretended not to, just to keep up the façade of disapproval. That, too, was tiring—pretending not to love Shelley as much as I did. There was too much about her that delighted me: the eloquence of her raised eyebrow after Dustin pointed out something particularly obvious; the books she read and left all over their house, in the bathroom, on the stairs. I loved that she read indiscriminately and that she'd talk with whoever she could about whatever book on American social policy she'd picked up or whichever Polynesian cookbook she'd found in the co-op's book donation bin. There were things about Shelley I wished were true about me and the fact that Dustin loved her without reserve made my self-loathing writhe up spiteful and mean.

Dustin pushed his hands back into the incision. Pressed against his back, I felt him fishing around in the cow. Suddenly he pulled his hands out again with the slick hooves of the calf in his fists. I felt a thrill. He counted, we pulled, and the nose gushed out. He counted again, and we all heaved together. The shoulders came out. So fast we stumbled back, the stomach, the hips and the hind legs shot out. The farmer fell back and caught himself on his hands. I fell back into his lap, and both of us struggled to stand up.

Dustin held fast to the hooves and the calf's head lolled back on his slippery red-furred body. "Help me get him over to the fence, Glen."

"Look at the size of him! He dead?"

"Yeah. Too big. Look at his head."

I saw it then—the swollen area behind the calf's ears, his bulbous pink nose, his long black lashes glued down with amniotic fluid to a grossly misshapen face. I stopped brushing myself off and stepped back. I stepped out of the stall, back into shadow, toward the cold wall of the barn, so that the activities in the aisle were behind me, like something happening far away and elsewhere. I leaned my forehead against the barn wall. I listened to Dustin and the farmer discuss the calf. The wife banged back into the barn, saying she hadn't been able to get her son on the phone. I heard her exclamations about the calf, piercing, like the yip of a small dog.

The calf looked like my worst pregnancy nightmares— the gruesome images I'd wake up with after sleep so deep I had to fight to come back to consciousness—encephalitis, bonelessness, missing limbs or organs or eyes. The unborn twins had been a joy to me in utero, and a pain, if I was honest, when they rolled around in my gut, but they'd terrified me, too. What if, after the vulnerability of pregnancy, there was just death? I thought of my boys' broad backs, their tousled hair, their dirty socks. I saw them sleeping and awake, from perfect, tiny newborns through to young men on the cusp of their first moustaches, sprawled on their backs in their boxer shorts, snoring, the appalling wispy trails of pubic hair leading into their baggy waistbands. Motherhood was loss.

I was cold inside my coat again. I felt like I might throw up, but I swallowed hard and knew I wouldn't. The wind blew against my face through the cracks. I heard my brother say, "He couldn't have lived. Too long inside and the womb can be a hostile environment. He's a bit soft now, see? He's just on the verge of rotten. I'll get your cow all cleaned up so she doesn't go rotten, too. Won't take long."

Motherhood was loss, but sisterhood was, too. In the car I'd said, "You always thought you knew how the story would turn out."

He'd said, "I usually did."

"You never did. You always thought they got home safe or you said how they weren't even having an adventure, they were only dreaming."

"Well, half the time they were."

"They never were. I thought they wouldn't get home. They had to be so brave and clever."

Dustin shook his head. "Well, they were."

I remembered it differently. "They weren't always. Remember how one of them died?"

"You're making that up."

"Seriously. I remember."

"Bullshit. He never told stories dark as that."

He did. I would swear on his grave once he had one. I'd stared out of the truck at the trees in the distance and beyond to Sinkut Mountain black on the horizon, and I remembered the time the brother had to bring the sister back from the dead. In 100 level Classics class at university, I'd recognized the story of Orpheus and Eurydice, sort of. The siblings, like the lovers, had been separated by sudden death—a snake bite, in both cases—but the brother could bring his sister back from the other side if he led them both up from hell without looking back. I remembered straining against the front seat, willing the kids to keep together, begging the big boy in the story not to give up hope, to know his sister was behind him. "Don't you remember?"

Dustin was quiet, his eyes on the road. There was silence in the car, just the tire hum, the night around us.

I'd given up. Then I heard him ask, "Was there singing?"

There was. The brother started a song they both knew and they sang their way up the hill of bones from the underworld into the light. It was a song we knew.

"Dad said their voices fit together like the strands of a rope, winding around itself until it was thick and golden and useful and they hauled on it until they were both lying in a heap on the grass in the sunshine, breathing and crying. Alive."

Dustin was quiet for a long moment. "Huh," was what he said. He flashed his high beams at a passing car to warn of black ice behind us.

When he'd called me with the news our parents had transferred ownership of everything to him—the practice, the house, the vehicles—it made logical sense. To me they gave an equivalent sum of money, but the difference between logic and emotion was too great. He was getting our childhood and I wasn't sure he cared enough about it, not the way I did. Our parents headed south in their brand-new Mercedes camper van, freed from the burden of land and practice, and it was easy to picture Mom every day, doing a crossword from a booklet with pages of the thinnest newsprint, her perfect silver curls bent over her work. Dad would be listening to the CBC, no matter where they were. He'd have it on satellite if need be. He'd play it loud and it would irritate Mom, but he'd do it anyway. I pictured the Grand Canyon, Polaroids of the two of them standing stylish in dark glasses on its rim, but those were real photos that existed of our grandparents on their honeymoon. Mom and Dad didn't have a Polaroid. Mom was in love with her phone camera. I could follow them on social media, but I didn't.

Throughout the year I drove the boys here and there, following paths I hefted into the Vancouver asphalt with my crossover SUV, hauling their sports equipment and their bodies all over kingdom come, and I did it willingly so that if I was ever asked I could say *of course, it's what you do for your kids*. And that was true, but was it enough? They hardly noticed the effort I went to and had gone to since they were small, keeping them alive, feeding their little brains, amusing them while we waited in doctor's offices. I'd always told them stories. I had stories bubbling in my chest all the time—the ones Dad had told us, but others too—stories of two brothers, kites and raptors, wilderness and danger. I wasn't sure if they ever really listened. When they were small they asked questions and hung on the outcome of each story, but was it worth anything? No, if Dustin was any example. He was so literal. I still half-believed the electric fence ran on fairy dust, just like Dad said.

In the cavern of my days, behind the windows of my eyes, I told myself stories in order to keep going—stories about the city and the people in it, stories about my children and who they'd grow up to be. I told myself stories of how I mattered, that I didn't need a vocation or a practice for my life to be worthwhile; it was obvious in the boys' strong white teeth, in Joe's sexual satisfaction, in the good healthy meals I cooked, that I was fine. I got everyone to their events on time. I kept up my appearance and stayed beautiful, though Joe didn't care. I was expert at fixing my makeup in the visor mirror, so quick with the concealer and mascara wand, and I never ran out of wet wipes because, though the crying always caught me by surprise, I'd be damned if I'd be caught at it.

I'd let Joe drive on our way north to Dustin's. I'd watched the rain turn to snow, the triple lanes become double lanes, become single lanes. I'd felt the climb up the province like I was pushing the truck from behind, and I wanted to quit, to let it roll all the way down to the coast and take me back to the home I'd made, the beautiful beige-and-linen living room and the way the sun poured in when it was gracious enough to do so. The worst part of the drive was turning in to our old driveway. I'd said nothing, so as not to dampen the joy of Joe and the boys. We drove past the familiar gate and trees and I knew every bump and pothole, even under the snow. I let the feeling of being a kid in this place rise up and engulf me. Little Celia and little Dustin came to life in my imagination and I felt that familiar sense of satisfaction, of being part of something, whole and totally unconcerned with the world outside of whatever we were up to.

I'd replaced that little girl with this capable grown-up carefully and completely when I understood it was all over, our childhood and our connection, Dustin's and mine, but suddenly it felt false. It strained my heart to keep up the invention, to pretend it didn't kill me to have grown up into someone I wouldn't want to have dinner with, let alone live with forever, when I'd thought it would all be so different. I wouldn't let it show, though. I gave my head a shake. I could pull off beautiful and well put-together for a week, or a lifetime. I could pull that shit off forever.

Dustin and I came in late Christmas night through the mudroom, shedding our snowy, barn-smelling coats and boots, entering the steamy kitchen where Shelley's fresh cookies cooled on a tray. They were all playing cards, drinking hot buttered rum or Cokes or tea, egging each other on, fighting about the rules, the boys a collective din that was almost unbearable.

Shelley struggled out of her chair, strained up on her tip-toes, and leaned past her belly to kiss Dustin on the mouth. I draped my arms around Joe in his chair from behind and buried my face in his neck—spiced rum and cinnamon on his breath when he laughed. We joined in, played until midnight, game after game, until both boys begged off, exhausted, explaining to their tipsy uncle that Santa wouldn't come if they didn't go to bed.

"Who says he's coming? Aren't you too old for that?"

Laughter, goodnights, one last drink, and then we all stumbled away, left the cups where they stood, found the cool of our pillows, and let the day end.

Joe and I lay as usual: Joe, the big spoon and me, the small. He was like a full-body heater and I needed it in the drafty room. I hoped the boys were warm enough in the basement, that they had enough blankets. I hoped they would sleep in, and then I hoped nothing. My breathing slowed and sleep crept nearer. I could feel it thick and woolen in the room.

Down the hall, from Mom and Dad's old room, I heard the floor creak and groan under Dustin and Shelley's feet. I heard Dustin's voice, a low rumble, and Shelley's high laugh, a little shout in the night, and I heard their bed thump the wall twice and then, though I listened, lazily, hardly awake, I heard nothing except Joe snoring softly like a cat. I was so tired, aching in my muscles, I thought I'd fall asleep instantly, but though I lay there, dazed and still, the farm call replayed in my brain. Details of the cow's wet curls plastered against her hocks, my brother, face against the cow's flank, shoulders-deep in the incision. I opened my eyes to stop the film reel, and stared at the dark. Sleep wouldn't come. I listened for noises beyond the familiar house noises. I listened and followed my breath in and out. I followed my mind up out of the bed to the door, through the crack, out into the cold hallway. Down the hall I went, past the stairway down to boys' room, where they slept leaden and still in the basement, and further down the hall to Dustin's room. Moments passed and I waited until a thin mist of him whispered out from under the door, through the dust on the floor and grew solid.

We were quiet and still for a second until, with a massive rush, we raced together down the hall, through the kitchen, out the mudroom, and through the cracks around the front door, children again, or a feeling of being a child, bare limbs in the summer heat.

Across the gravel driveway we flew, clattering on summer-hard soles, clambering up the end of the cattle chute, all leg-churn and muscle burn. We rattled down the boards avoiding the cow pies, the rough wood of the two narrow fences that hemmed the cattle in holding us in now, zebra-striping us in the yard light, and, before it swallowed us into its darkness, we felt the rush of cold wind from the open door of the large animal clinic where the chute let its captives free. The large animal clinic, perpetually cool in its cinderblock darkness, echoed around us. We raced for the door handle, dodging puddles on the floor, avoiding the great big grate in the centre of the room, fearing the possibility of our father having parked the car in there (the time Dustin knocked himself out on the door of it, Dad having left it open to air). We rammed flat into the far wall in front of the sink, sending the light fixtures groaning on their chains.

The door was locked. When was the door ever locked? We couldn't get in. We milled about in the dark, before I remembered the laundry room, the old dusty furnace room above it and the vent we'd dropped pennies through into the exam room below.

We roared through the quiet where there used to be thumping, rattling washing machines, the scent of fabric softener, for washing the dog blankets and mop heads, up the wooden ladder against the concrete and into the hot still place we'd once thought to build a hideout until we couldn't stand the heat and came out covered in red, bumpy, insulation prickles. We peered through the vent into the exam room—quiet out of habit, we'd be sent home if we were loud, if we asked too many questions—saw the shine on the exam table, the glass jars of long Q-tips and syringes and cotton balls. We crept through the waiting room along the floor, under the plastic chairs where we were never allowed to play, through the forest of metal chair legs. We could leap over the desk into the reception area or steal through exam room two, but we wanted the office, anticipating its wonders: hot chocolate powder and the horse pelt layered over the creaky wooden rolling chair, the box with the rubber heart with heartworms squiggling through it in white ribbons, the way both of us could fit under the desk with a popsicle and not have to come out until work was over and we'd all go home, hand-in-hand with Dad. We went and waited under the desk, careful to be quiet and still in the dark, watching dust settle in moonbeams streaming through the windows. We waited while the current built inside us, little wisps of bright yellow, little sparks of cobalt and cornflower blue. We waited until suddenly we bolted and we were down the linoleum hallway in a heartbeat, past the medicine fridge, past the shelves of little boxes full of pills and vials, past the bins of magnets for pulling nails out of the bellies of cows or some other mysterious purpose that we didn't know, magnets we lined up in long trains the length of the hallway before the animal health technician would yell at us and make us go home. We zoomed past the cold operating room, past the X-ray room and its captivating stink of developing fluid, into the small animal kennel room, right into a kennel, slamming the door behind us. The metal bathtub rang with the clang of the metal doors, the force popping the latch up and closed so we were locked in a six-by-six-by-three-foot concrete and metal cage, the top of it mesh, a drain in the sloped floor below.

We pulsed, hearts throbbing in the dark, waiting again, but for what? We were two children squeezed into a metal cage for Great Danes and orphaned colts. I climbed the gate and dropped onto Dustin like a wrestler from the top rope. He bounced up from the painted floor, flailing, hollering, and I fought him, smashing and biting, kicking and flailing, until he shot through the door, using the trick of the flat hand sideways slipping the gate latch up that had taken years for us to perfect, and we tumbled out into the room, spent, and rested on the cool floor, done for the moment, still. Out of habit, we peered under the stacked kennels for a sight of Tommy, the runaway turtle, but she wasn't there. She never was. We might have made her up.

I felt his heat at my elbow where his elbow nearly touched mine. I felt him waiting for me to make a move or for something to happen or me to leave so he could chase me again. Neither of us moved. When the furnace roared on we rose in unison and stepped out the back door into the bright light of the moon.

We drifted together to the tall, tall swings, me toward my favourite—the one with the white seat—and him toward the black-seater, both of us dreamy, wanting for the swoop and drop, the lean and soar, the graceful arc of the swings our father built when we were almost too old for them that we loved anyway, that we gravitated to as teenagers, where we could talk without fighting, where we felt young and old both because we were on the cusp of life and knew it suddenly. We knew this time was short, though it hadn't seemed so before, back in the treehouse, back at the creek, in the dark of our shared bedroom when we laughed ourselves to sleep at some stupid thing one or the other of us said.

We rested on the seats. In my dream I climbed up the shining chains, and Dustin followed up his, and we rested on the very top of the swingset, a swingset the height of telephone poles since that's what our father had bought to build it, and looked out at our home, the acres we'd known right down to the individual grass stem, the muddy bottom of the trout pond we'd learned with our feet, the old green boat we'd sunk accidentally, then turned over to use as an island to throw rocks from for ten summers until we both couldn't fit on its turtled back. We looked out at the tree tops and the field. We watched the house spurting furnace smoke into the sky and waited. But for what?

I was still waiting, lying on my back in the dark. I'd thought we'd love each other, know each other, need each other like that until we were dead. I hadn't seen it would change. I never knew I'd be half a person for my whole adult life, that being a wife wouldn't fix it and being a mother had nothing to do with it. I mourned every day for something I'd never heard anyone else acknowledge, least of all my brother. What was this feeling but selfish and indulgent? I could wait all night or for my whole life and it wouldn't come back. It didn't even matter.

I watched our dream selves drop slowly from the sky, two shining children, and when we reached the roof of the house, we fell, suddenly, and shattered in the driveway. Flecks of gold in the gravel. Particles of dust.

I must have slept. At dawn on Christmas morning I found Dustin eating cereal from a small mixing bowl at the kitchen table.

"Any left for me?"

He pushed the milk toward me, indicating the bowl cupboard with a nod of his head. I filled a bowl with flakes and poured milk over them.

"No sugar?"

"Diabetes," I said, knowing I didn't have to explain. Diabetes was Dad's bogeyman.

Dustin filled his bowl again and topped it with a lump from the sugar jar, maybe deliberately, maybe trying to make me smile.

We ate in silence until I was finished. He pointed with his chin at the whisky bottle and raised his eyebrows at me. Christmas morning the sun passed the yardarm at daybreak, Dad used to say, and he put whisky in every drink he had until we poured his body into bed before the carnage of Christmas dinner was even cleared. I poured myself a drink, feeling cheeky and sad at the same time.

I drew my legs up to rest my feet on the next chair over. I leaned my head back so my hair fell away from my face and said, "Hey, remember that time I was helping Dad with a post-mortem in the yard and I had to hold the cow's leg up after he cut her open, and he and the farmer were talking, and it was so heavy, and my hand was all bloody and it slipped and I dropped the leg and it fell and smashed the cow shut and guts and dead cow sprayed over everyone?" I smiled.

"That was me."

"What?" I put my feet down and sat up. "No, that was me. The leg was super heavy. I remember my arm shaking and thinking I should use two hands and right then my fingers slipped."

"It was me. You were in the house."

I put my palms on the table and stood up. "What are you talking about? That was me, I dropped the leg..."

"No. You were watching from your room. I remember I looked back at the house and you were standing in your bedroom window holding the curtain aside, laughing at me."

And it was true. Suddenly I knew. I remembered the blue cotton of the curtain Mom had made in my right hand, my left hand on the window casing. I'd just opened it. I was looking through the screen. I could hear Dad yelling. I watched Dustin cower, back up to the edge of the bed of the pickup truck and jump off into the driveway. I watched the farmer take out his hankie and wipe the blood off his face. I watched Dad stand and follow Dustin to the edge of the truck bed, yelling, flicking guts off his coverall with both hands. I saw Dustin glance up at me, but I wasn't laughing. I could smell the cow's stomach, the blood and shit mixing with the hay in the truck bed. I could feel the summer sun on my hair, on Dustin's hair, the pit in my stomach, the shame bringing the heat to the surface of our skin.

"Oh my God, that was you." I remembered the truck driving off after, the thin trails of red and green, blood and shit, streaming out the back of the truck onto the driveway, and then the highway. I'd found Dustin chucking chunks of clay into the pond afterward.

He snorted. "You always do that. Take my memories." He laughed a little more. "Who do you think you are?"

I sat back down in my chair. "I don't even know."

"That wasn't a serious question." He shook the cereal box to see how much it held.

"I mean it. I have no idea. It exhausts me." My voice shrank as I said it, getting smaller and smaller. "I feel like if I let go and start crying, I'll never be able to stop. Like all the tears in the world won't fix me."

Dustin didn't notice. "That's not what tears do. It's just a physiological response to remove irritants. They're to wash your eyeballs free of grit, to lubricate..."

"Dustin, stop. Are you seriously going to lecture me? Did you not hear what I said? I'm telling you something I wouldn't tell anyone, and I don't want your scientific instruction!"

We stared at each other. The low light from the range hood hit the grey in his hair and turned his eyes black. We stared at each other and my eyes filled and brimmed over. We were strangers. I had to accept it. He looked away. He chewed and swallowed, and I wiped my face with my sleeves.

I was going to get up. I was going to leave the room and go somewhere he wasn't. I stood, ready with a retort, so it startled me when he reached across to where I'd set my hand on the table. His huge mitt, as Mom called it, hovered over the back of my hand and I could feel the heat of him, an incredible heat radiating out of his palm. I pictured him laying it down on top of mine, gentle, like when he'd touched the cow in the barn to say *hey there, I'm here, I'm not going anywhere*, but he didn't. I looked at his hand. I looked at my hand. I looked at the space between them.

The night before I'd stood still in the middle of the tumult lit bright as morning by the bare bulb's light. I'd watched Dustin stoop and put away his kit, his movements fast and efficient, his system of order apparent even in his field case which, though dusty with hay chaff, was tidy and organized; his instruments shone, the light flashed off the plastic wrappers of needles and suture material. I'd watched him tidy up, scrubbing his hands and arms in the soapy, bloody water for the hundredth time, his pink scalp shining bald and bright on the top of his head. I'd just noticed it, the tiny bald spot. It made me tender toward him. I picked up his heavy black case and carried it for him.

He'd stopped as we followed the farmers out of the barn. "I wish Shelley could see this," he'd said, looking around him at the smooth and white world. "Sometimes I wish she knew all the stuff we saw and did as kids."

I stopped. The world stopped. It was an abrupt turn, but I'd been waiting for it. I'd been waiting all my adult life for him to acknowledge what we'd had. I'd thought I might start crying.

"Then she'd know why I'm so weird." He shrugged. Sighed out a white cloud.

I didn't cry then. I didn't do anything. The wind blew. It was Christmas Eve and we stood together in the snow, Dustin's words dissipating into the black satin of the sky, and for the first time I could imagine my life without the weight of waiting for him to need me again.

I stepped past him, eventually, walking with my face tucked into the collar of my coat. I led the way down the path toward the truck, stumbling in the prints we'd made hours earlier which were indistinct, half-filled with blown snow. Around me, the night felt massive and empty.

At the truck, I pulled open the back door for him. He nodded his thanks and put his bucket inside. I set the case beside it. We walked around, each to our respective sides, and got in. He started it up and we drove slowly, lurching side to side on the rutted road, back the way we'd come. The light from the barn spilled meagrely out onto the ground so the snow looked split and broken into black chasms in front of us, but Dustin ploughed on, slow and steady, his eyes forward, sure of the road even in the dark.

NIGHT WATCH

Tom's eyes are shut against the light, or to keep the dust out, or to pray. Who knows? He sits in the wood chair they found in a ditch and dragged home to the little brick patio Hugh built for this purpose: so Tom could sit in the sun between appointments, watching birds and listening to the highway traffic. In the winter, Tom felt the big burly semi-trucks grinding backward through their gears to slow up for town, trucks carrying sea cans and loads of chipped wood that they humped across-province, from the coast in the west, following the rivers east, to the Fraser, where they'd make a hard right and head for Vancouver. Now buds are beginning on the aspen and he can smell dog shit and last year's leaves thawing in the puddles that dot the yard.

Tom feels the heat of the sun drip down his hair, into his scalp, onto his neck and shoulders. He isn't listening to anything—bird or truck. He deliberately keeps his brain blank so he doesn't have to relive the Paltrow's cocker spaniel pissing on his exam table, making a mess Janelle swore about when she saw. He tries to let nothing of the day, or the past days, seep in to taint the morning, but his lack of sleep makes it difficult.

Hugh has made a sandwich for Tom, something he's never done before. On weekends, Tom builds masterful sandwiches with tomato and bacon, dill pickles quartered lengthways on the side, and delivers them to Hugh at the kitchen table. Today, Hugh has cobbled together some-thing special from the cupboard: kippers, mashed with salt and pepper on buttered bread with cucumber slices. He has a beer in each pocket of Tom's jacket, which he's appropriated for the journey across the muddy yard from the house to the clinic. He's only made one sandwich. He isn't hungry. He is intent. He has something to say.

"Hi sweetie, I brought you a little sandwich."

Tom startles, sits up fast. He may have been sleeping a little. The inside of his mouth has dried out.

"And I brought drinks." Hugh puts the plateful of sandwich into Tom's hands and sits on the milk crate they use as a patio coffee table. He holds a beer out to Tom, who isn't yet sure what to do with the sandwich. He blinks, trying to catch up.

"Hugh, it's morning. I can't have a beer. There's a dog with quills coming at eleven-thirty."

"Fine." Hugh puts both beers down on the patio and gets out his cigarettes.

Tom lifts the top of the sandwich and looks at the cucumbers. Hugh lights up, inhales, watches his boyfriend re-lid the sandwich and sniff it.

"It's kippers," he says. "It's what was in the cupboard."

"I've never had kippers before. Did you buy them?"

"No, I don't eat kippers. Jesus. They must have been here since before. Since Dr. What's-His-Name."

"McLennan." Tom speaks through a bite, careful to keep the food in his mouth. It's actually good—salty and rich, and the cucumbers are fresh.

"Listen," Hugh says. He stubs out his cigarette half-finished, leans forward, then away. He says, "I think we should talk."

Tom looks toward the highway. The heat of the sun seeps into his sweater. The salty fish in his mouth, the butter. Cucumbers were a great idea. He smiles at Hugh, chews, swallows, takes another bite. Doesn't answer.

Tom walks to reception with his head in a file and trips on a German Short-haired Pointer. It yelps and scampers under the desk.

"Janelle, is this your dog?" He peers under the desk. It's young. It doesn't make another sound.

"Yeah. That's Teapot Mountain. He's okay, but don't touch him. He nips." She comes in with two mugs of tea, sets them on the desk, and peers underneath with Tom.

"Teapot what?"

"Mountain. I heard of a dog called Mississippi and a cousin named her daughter Brooklyn, so I thought I'd name him after a place. My sister boards her horse near there."

"Brooklyn?"

"No, Teapot Mountain. There's a lookout at the top."

"He's piddling."

"Damn. I'm trying to get him to stop that." Janelle grabs the paper towel from the dispenser over the sink. She rips off pieces and lays them on the pee.

"He's really sweet, I think."

"He is, when he's not biting."

Tom finds the tea on the desk and brings the cup to his lips. It says PUSHING 40 on one side and BETTER THAN PUSHING UP DAISIES on the other. "Is this for me?"

"Course it is. Who else is it for? You see anyone else here?" Janelle drops into her chair, turns back to the open files on her desk. She hands the one on top to Tom. Teapot Mountain walks four times in a circle and lies down on her feet. "Your four-thirty will be here in a minute. Drink up."

Tom takes his tea with him. The last dog she rescued she gave to a customer without letting Tom know in advance. He considers getting a cookie to lure this one into the office to sleep under his desk, but he shouldn't get attached. Beautiful eyes, Teapot Mountain. And nice shiny coat. He's healthy.

The bell on the front door jangles and the door snaps shut again. Voices. He swills his tea, puts it down half-drunk, and slips his arms into the lab coat he grabs off the office door.

TWICE IN ONE NIGHT

Two prolapsed uterus calls, back to back.

FIRST, SECOND, THIRD

Mr. Barlow says there is something wrong with his dog. It does this weird thing where it won't poop in the yard, so it holds it until he gets home. And when he takes it for a walk, it yelps when it finally poops, then poops at least two more times before it's really finished. "She sounds like I'm taking the boots to her."

Tom lets Poppy the Dalmatian walk around the exam room so he can watch her move. She sniffs his boots and pant legs. He palpates her belly, stroking her silky black and white fur. She waggles her hind end at the attention.

"What's the stool look like?"

"Well, the first one is like a bunch of rocks. Once as big as a lacrosse ball. Gross. The second one is softer, like reasonable. And the third is a write-off. No one's gonna pick that shit up. Runny. Diarrhoea."

"Colour?" Tom feels the dog's underbelly. He squeezes her innards gently, watching her keep waggling, not wincing.

"Like I said, gross."

Tom raises his eyebrows at Mr. Barlow—a request for more, please.

"Number one, black, number two, brown, number three, light brown and disgusting."

"Okay. That's good to know." Tom squats down to peer in the dog's eyes. He's stroking the dog to keep her happy and near to him, but he's listening to Janelle outside the door answer the phone at the reception desk. He can't hear what she's saying, but he gets the feeling he's going out this afternoon. He pulls the dog's lips back to check her gums, then he slips his fingers around her muzzle, pressing her lips onto her teeth so she opens her mouth. He studies her tongue. Janelle has her notation voice going—methodical, taking directions, he's sure, to a farm. He feels his afternoon change, all the appointments disappearing one by one. Janelle will collect the animals as they come in, he'll head out, and when he gets back, after whatever calving mayhem awaits him, he'll do the spays and check-ups and neuters and teeth extractions and tail-dockings or whatever else is necessary in the evening, after hours, to catch up. Hugh won't be happy. He'd said something about ribs for supper.

"Doctor?"

"Hmmm?" Tom scoops Poppy up in his arms and puts her on the exam table. He's got his stethoscope in his ears before he answers Barlow's question. "What was that?"

"You think it's a real problem?" Barlow has hair like a scarecrow's under his toque, like someone had constructed his hair out of hay stubble. His eyes are sad. He reaches out a hand and rests it on the dog's back.

"No, I don't. I think it might be a quirk of hers and it may be something you have to live with, but it could be something you manage with food, too. What do you feed her?"

"Dry food we get at the grocery store. Sometimes leftovers."

Tom doesn't expect any different. In fact, he's quit listening. Janelle has pushed her chair back from her desk. He hears the roll of its wheels on the lino, the click of Teapot Mountains' nails as he follows her to the door. Janelle knocks.

"Tom? You're wanted on line one."

If he's wanted on the phone, it's bad. Janelle comes in, smiles at Barlow and puts her hand alongside his on the dog's back. She fits her body in beside the table just as Tom extracts his, leaving no gap, no change in presence for the animal. They make a good team.

"What's left?" She's still smiling at Barlow but she says it to Tom.

"Temperature. Food suggestions. That's it. Thanks, Janelle. I'll see you later, Mr. Barlow, and you, Poppy." He pats the dog, nods at her owner and leaves the room, carefully pulling the door to behind him. He feels the change in the day and it feels like freedom and servitude both, but it's not unpleasant. He feels it like a shift in the weather, in his sinuses, his mood. He takes the phone call in his office, already shrugging off his lab coat.

"Tom Gunn, here. How can I help?"

Tom stands in six inches of manure and straw considering his options. The red-brown sides of the heifer, distended around her calf, heave with each breath. She's panting, lowing, shaking her head, spittle hanging down from her mouth. Tom has one hand in this coverall pocket fingering an agate he found earlier and the other hanging slack, encased in a poop-smeared plastic glove from armpit to fingertips.

"We have some choices."

The farmer spits into the hay. "Probably not good ones."

"No." Tom shifts his weight, watches the cow sway. "Not good ones."

He walks around to the back of her and thinks about the size of her pelvis. "Charolais bull, right?"

"I know, I know. I got greedy. Didn't think about the size of the cow."

"Bet she wishes you did."

The farmer grins, and spits again.

"Well, if you're gonna ship her anyway," Tom looks to the farmer, who nods, "then it's just a matter of getting the calf out, no worries about a next time for breeding."

"And the calf's alive?" The farmer is hopeful.

"So far."

"So how we gonna do it?"

Tom shakes his head, walks into the gloom near the doorway where he's left his kit. "Calf puller. Chains didn't work, no luck with manual extraction, so puller it is."

"And if that doesn't work?"

"Caesarean."

"Damn." The farmer spits. Tom walks back into the light with his metal pole and breech. Brutal, that's what he thinks. Brutal, but necessary. A pole, a breech, a ratchet, and chains. Simple. Awful. He pats the cow's red curls, says, "Hold on, boss."

It's the worst night of a farmer's life. Or close to it. No one wants to call the vet. It's too expensive. It's not something someone budgets for. You only call the vet for an act of God, an unnatural disaster. You call the vet because you can't handle events yourself, and no one wants to admit that.

Tom is used to breaching private space, to pulling into a barnyard past where the family's cars are parked, stopping to get out and open the gate, then stopping again to close it behind him. He's used to waiting for someone to open a tricky latch or unlock a gate so he can drive up to the barn, park closer with his equipment. He's not a guest, but he's a guest of honour in that old men defer to him, men with fifty years' experience running a ranch in the middle of nowhere, who've handled scenes of mayhem they didn't show Tom in vet school. Tom's the one with the drugs, though, the skill with a scalpel, the knowledge in his gut and fingertips of which organ it is he feels in the cow's dark insides. He's the last resort. He's a knight in shitty armour. He's an expensive nuisance. He's going to say ship the cow or save her. He's a man the farm wives pity, out at all hours, no woman to make him breakfast or dinner, whatever he needs. He's the one the old cowboys laugh at because he never seems to get their dirty jokes, he's so proper or polite or whatever it is, smart or stupid, that he doesn't get it, so they laugh around him while he works. But if a man's on his own, and if it's been a long night or an awful night and he's tried everything and nothing worked, Tom will talk low and quiet and let him know his options, reassure him—say that he did the best he could, that so-and-so out by Finmoore had the same problem and lost both calf and cow and there's a chance tonight they might be able to save one or both of them. Tom never gossips. Farmers appreciate the information. They need to know they're not the only one whose calves have scours. They need to know these night visits aren't exclusive to their farm. It might be the first time they see Doc Gunn this season or it might be the fifth time and they want to kill him for still being kind when they feel like idiots for having to call for help.

Some consider calling Jones during pregnancy-testing season in the fall because he does it for cheap, but he's not an expert, despite what he says. Jones is just some ass who thinks a vet's job is something anyone can do, who wants to make a few bucks on the side, whose own herd had pretty good odds when he preg-tested them himself, so his track record's not bad.

Ole Siggurdson, the farmer who told him, said Doc Gunn just shrugged when he heard about it. Ole felt a bit of a snitch letting him know, but he likes the guy, his cowlick and downcast eyes. Just let him know out of kindness. Probably wasn't even the Doc called the association—that was likely someone else. Gunn's above that stuff. Young Doc the vet, with his shitty Bronco, his willingness to drop everything and come, no matter how far out your place is. And he's not a drunk, like the old vet was. Gunn's not like that. He's good folk, despite what they say about him and that roommate of his. Some folks say he's gay, but that's none of anyone's business. Bit of a Bible belt around here, but Tom Gunn, DVM, has been welcomed in. Young Doctor Gunn. From away, but a good sort. He's a thorough doctor, and his preg-testing record's nothing to laugh at.

TOM TAKES A BREAK

He locks the door behind him. The floor creaks and a dog out in the kennel room howls in reply. Tom drops his pants and boxers, sits on the toilet and closes his eyes. There's no fan in this old bathroom, in this old house he bought and connected to its neighbour with cinderblocks to make a twenty by twenty room with a garage door and a squeeze in it he uses for a large animal clinic. He nearly dislocates his shoulder prying the window open from his seated position.

He'd found the two war-time houses with their drooping porches when he first arrived in Hulatt. They were too cheap to pass up, and right on the edge of town—less than the cost of a duplex in Vancouver with six acres between them, and frontage on the highway. He bought the third house in the row to live in. Nine acres, total. He was already settled in by the time he met Hugh. Hugh arrived and they'd finished the chicken run and coop together, though Hugh was vocally skeptical about the place and why anyone would voluntarily live there. Tom finished the barn himself, last fall, right before the first hard frost. He loves every aspect of the place. There is something delightful about walking from the old parlour in the south house, through the door, across the concrete floor and over the drain of the large animal clinic, into the low-ceilinged kitchen of the north house, where he'd put the reception area. The plumbing's awful, though. The pipes freeze, the taps howl, and the water pressure makes Hugh swear through his morning showers.

Tom tries to relax. He's got about four and a half minutes to shit. Four and a half minutes behind a closed door. He takes out his undergrad English anthology of poetry and opens it to the bookmark. Tennyson. He takes a deep breath and lets the wonder roll through him. The first dog's howls set off a chain reaction of howling and barking. Five dogs singing in captivity: two recovering from neuters, waiting for pick up, one poor puppy in isolation yipping despite its weakness after parvo, and two dogs on the south side of the room adding their voices to the mix—one after whelping and one who'd had an intimate introduction to the bumper of a car at the corner of 5th and Stuart yesterday morning.

Tom feels his bowels move as they were meant to, happy because of the dogs and the poetry, and because doing it now means he won't have to worry about it later when he's on the road between farms with no toilet in sight. Warm air blasts from the wall heaters and the pipes sing. The dogs bark. Tom places his bookmark and gets ready to rejoin the morning.

TOM CAN'T KEEP HIS EYES OPEN

It's so important not to shut the eyes, not to let the lids sink, not to drop. Off. To sleep. Tom sits up straighter in the seat of the Bronco. He inhales deeply, then exhales. He lifts his shoulders, shrugs them, shakes them out, all while keeping his eyes tight to the white line. He's not going to fall asleep. He rolls the window down a bit. It's fresher. He takes another breath, holds it, then lets it out in a whistle. *Stay awake*. It's nine-thirty at night. He's been awake since four in the morning. He's seen about a billion dogs and cats, a turtle, and a ferret. He missed lunch and supper. The farm call that started at six just finished. He has to stay awake only ten kilometres longer and then he can fall asleep in the driveway if he wants to. He could sleep all night in the Bronco. If he slept in the truck, Janelle wouldn't find him in the morning, he wouldn't have to answer the phone and get called out to some other calving tomorrow. And another and another. He's done twenty since February. It's March now. Flurries of snow scud across the highway, flare white in his headlights and disappear off the roadside. Tom opens his mouth as wide as he can. He stretches his jaw from side to side. He nods exaggeratedly, all while keeping his eyes on the white line. He drove off the road last spring. He's not doing that again. *Awake, awake, awake, awake, awake.* Hugh said, "Don't die," when Tom rolled out of bed to go see that heifer this morning. Hugh said, "Stay awake." Tom's staying awake. He unzips his coat, hits himself on the chest. He sings *Doo wop a loo bop, she's my baby* in the loudest, lowest voice he can muster. He couldn't save the calf, but he saved the cow. The calf was dead. They tore it apart with the calf-puller. Cranked the front end right out and left the back end behind, and then he'd had to fish it out with chains slipped over the little black hooves he'd hunted for inside the cow. *Doo wop a loo bop*! Tom has never sworn on a farm call. He says "heckin" and "fudgecicles." He's clean cut. He runs a tight ship. He doesn't overcharge. He never says yes to single malt, always says yes to tea back at the house. Tom stretches his right arm out and hooks his hand behind the passenger seat headrest and pushes to feel the muscles strain. He hangs his tongue out and barks. Blinks. Five more kilometres. He still feels like puking after the farm call tonight. He feels like he wants to stop the truck and cry. He gives himself a pep talk: he's good with money. He doesn't beat around the bush. He's young, but people trust him. He can keep a secret. He sympathizes if a man cries when he has to shoot his horse because it broke its leg, he looks away if a fellow needs to cry. He'd never hold that against someone. He never holds a grudge. He could hold his breath for thirty-two seconds as a child underwater... His tire rumbles on the rumble strip. *Dang it.* Tom jerks the wheel to the left. His tire on the rumble strip again. *Dang it.* Jerks the wheel. Tire on the strip, off the strip, in the dirt. *Fucksake*! Jerks the wheel, almost hits an oncoming truck. Jerks it back. He can see his gate. His own driveway up there on the highway. *Blink, Tom, blink.* He puts his blinker on, rumbles into the driveway, whimpering with relief. Pulls up behind the large animal clinic and turns the Bronco off. He lets his head drop onto the steering wheel, not sleeping, not crying, just finally still for a moment. Breathing wet and hard, snot dripping onto his lap. Even if he was crying, no one around to see him anyway.

HUGH CAN'T WORK LIKE THIS

He's fitting brown Lego together. Light brown, dark brown. He's building a larger-than-life cow. He and Tom bought five hundred dollars worth of Lego at the Walmart in the city and now he's fitting it together. Five hundred dollars worth of Lego is less than you'd think. Two and a half days drawing and calculating how to build a Jersey cow with eyes twice as large as a normal cow's, and a body in proportion to that. He will still have to buy some pink for the udder. Thank god Lego comes in bins pre-sorted by colour. It's soothing, in a way, reaching into the bin, pulling out a piece, looking at the instructions he's made, and fitting it together—like being seven, home sick from school. But Hugh can't work like this. The guest room is too small. The whole project is bigger than he's even figured out, yet. He's mad at Tom. He has to pry the bricks apart and try again. He's mad at Tom for not buying a proper farm with a big barn. Hugh could work in a barn. He's mad at Tom for buying the place in Hulatt, a ridiculously small town in central BC, hours from any reasonably-sized city. He's mad at Tom for not being a small animal vet in Vancouver—they could make so much money! He could go to shows. Openings. Galleries. He's mad at himself for agreeing to this. He wishes he didn't even like Tom. Tom with his green eyes, his hairless chest and surprisingly muscled forearms. Tom with shoulders like an Adonis. Tom with kindness flowing out of him as naturally as breath while Hugh sits here stinking mad in a tiny guest room that would fit no guest because he's filled it with cow, and now he's got to go back to the Walmart for pink blocks. When Tom gets paid. Because lord knows Hugh doesn't have any money, not with the fucking Canada Council shit-canning his application again this year. He needs more black, too.

Hugh rakes his hand through the Lego bin, the noise a soothing, deafening rattle he remembers from boyhood. He wonders if Tom would feel soothed by it, too, if he'd had Lego as a kid. Weird they haven't talked about that— he knows about Tom trying to fix up squashed frogs and snakes with tape and paper towel, him making his mother buy cooked chickens at the grocery store so he could cut them up and figure out how they work, but he can't actually picture Tom as a child. He remembers the first time he saw him at the vet conference in Vernon. Hugh was tending bar when Tom came in with a gaggle of badly-dressed, balding, middle-aged men. They sat with some cowboy-looking women—tight jeans and snap-button shirts—near the bar, and it was clear to Hugh they had money, the way they were ordering drinks, but they weren't businesspeople and they weren't dentists, the usuals who attended conferences at the off-season ski hill where he worked.

Hugh couldn't take his eyes off Tom. All the women at the table were ogling him, too, but Tom was oblivious. When Tom came up to the bar to buy his round, Hugh felt all fluttery. He tried to keep his eyes on the bar cloths he was folding, but Tom's farm-boy-good-looks, his forearms popping out of his rolled-up shirt sleeves, his lopsided grin and cowlick - Hugh took it all in. It was just a matter of getting hold of himself, of listening to Tom's faltering order, when he realized Tom was going to pay then sneak off to bed and Hugh might never see him again. Hugh made the decision to woo him. A little joke to get past Tom's shyness, and Hugh found out they were vets, so then a made up a story about a roommate's sick parrot. He asked Tom if he'd take a look at it after Hugh got off shift. Tom was confused by the parakeet in molt he'd found when they got to Hugh's place, but Hugh still feels he'd done what he had to in order to keep Tom from disappearing.

Hugh absently fits two brown bricks together. He'd told Tom everything about himself that night. Everything, and Tom still hadn't run away. Tom knows all his childhood stuff, all about his shitty exes and missteps and unattended art shows and one-night-stands, and he still loves Hugh. And Hugh knows it. He drops the Lego, pushes the bin away. It's arbitrary, all of it—life. He could have let Tom order his drinks and disappear, but he'd made a decision. And here he fucking is in Hulatt B.C. Wherever that is.

ENOUGH TIME TO DAYDREAM

Tom knew two things coming out of vet school: he wasn't going to practice in Saskatchewan, and he wasn't going to work for anyone else. He bought his practice sight unseen and moved out to the Nechako River valley the week after graduation. He'd worked near the area for a practicum the summer between third and fourth years and he'd loved it. He still does.

It's a blue blazer day—high sky, sun on fresh snow, middle of March and no sign of spring. Sure, some melt, but always another dump of snow. He's glad the deep freeze of February is over. His first winter, he couldn't believe it: he'd go from a heated barn to one with two-inch gaps between the boards and he'd plunge both arms into a cow's Caesarean incision to try to warm up.

He's got another half an hour before he gets to Martin's. Cow down with milk fever. Enough time to daydream. Enough time to count the raptors on the phone lines. Copse of white birch. This time of year is the best—bare tree limbs and birds galore, creeks eating through the ice, the black water rising, flushing over the rotten ice, water birds coming back to enjoy it.

He roars along at a hundred and twenty kilometres an hour, highway driving, spirits up despite the lack of sleep.

In the calf pen, waiting for him, are two calves given to Tom in trade, a big white fellow and a doe-eyed jersey calf. And in the old shed—into which he'd put a water trough, a feed trough, a heat lamp, and fresh straw each week—is a donkey, a stunted grey lady. He feeds the calves early in the morning from formula he mixes up in a big rubber bucket with warm water. He decants this into two stainless steel buckets, each with a white rubber nipple at the base like a cock standing proud in the morning. The donkey gets no milk substitute, only grain mixed with minerals that he shares out for all three in the feed trough.

There is pleasure in the smell of the oats and kernels, the rough wood of the fence and trough, the eager way the calves greet him. He lets them snuffle his hands. He gets into the pen and they bunt up against his legs, their hot animal bodies warming him, the red glow of the heat lamp turning them all livid and garish.

The donkey is standoffish. The calves can't get enough of him. He scratches their nubs of horns and behind their ears while they suck from the bucket, snorting and smearing snot all over the place, wild with the smell of the artificial milk. He checks their hooves out of habit, and their ears. He feels their furry bodies for unusual lumps or spots where the fur is worn away—anything odd or off.

Today, once they're done glugging nutrients, instead of rushing out, he sits down in the pen, slides down the rough boards until his rump is on the straw and lets the calves nose around his hair and ears and into his collar. He doesn't have time to, but he listens to them breathe. He breathes.

He is neck-deep in calving season. He is drowning in it. He doesn't know if he can keep it up. How much sleep do humans actually need? He lets his breath out and sucks another breath in. From the smell of it, he will need to change the straw soon. Or his clothes.

He watches the donkey watch him. It takes a step closer but stops if Tom moves. He rests his head on the board behind him. The donkey takes another step. The calves wander off, one to the water trough, and the other gets a leg into the feed trough then hops right up into it and kneels on its forelegs. It eats the grain from between its knock-knees. He laughs, and the donkey stops, suddenly two feet closer.

He should get up and go in for breakfast. He has to feed the chickens, yet. He'll have to check the phone—he heard it ringing as he was putting on his coverall. He fishes an agate out of his pocket where it bulges uncomfortably against his leg. Rough surface, innards like caught water. He holds it up to the morning light just starting to come in the plastic covered window of the shed, and the inside of the agate is frozen air, solid thought, a womb with no embryo. He folds his fingers around it, a lumpy perfect fit in his palm, and the donkey is suddenly right in front of him. It noses his closed fist, all velour and sandpaper. Wet breath on his face.

"Fancy meeting you here," he whispers.

She stares him in the eye—her liquid, chestnut orb so close he can see each individual lash plus himself reflected. She stomps and shakes her head, which makes him smile. He reaches out to rub her fur, but she sidles off to the corner again. He sighs. She was named Lacey, after the dead wife of the farmer who dropped her off in the fall; the donkey had lived in his yard for twenty years, but he was moving to the Okanagan. Tom gets a lot of animals that way: turtles some kid's grown out of, birds ousted once the family bought a cat. Once, he'd received a full-sized white Icelandic pony—he gave it away to a little girl in love with unicorns.

He watches the animals live their lives. The big calf sucks the jersey's tail through the slots of the food trough while she licks up the last of the grain. The donkey eyes him from afar, then turns her head to watch him out of the other eye. He notices a squint in it he doesn't like. He stands slowly and steps carefully toward her. He can see her ready to bolt, though she wouldn't have far to go in the small space, so he leaps with a knee forward and pins her to the fence. She struggles, but he has her. He leans close, using the weight of his body to keep her still, which frees both hands so he can inspect the eye. He knows what it is before he slides his hands around to check the lymph nodes at the back of her jaw. The swelling doesn't surprise him, but the tears that spring to his eyes do. Poor Lacey. Squamous Cell Carcinoma. Her eye weeping yellow and wet. He strokes her face and lets her go and she scrabbles to get away from him. He slaps the hair from his hands off on his coverall and wipes his own wet eyes. He steps over the fence, picks up the dirty buckets, and opens the shed door. He has to push himself to step out into the new morning light.

HUGH THINKS THAT SOUNDS LIKE PISSING

Hugh sits straight up in bed. It fucking is. "Tom! Stop! That's the closet!" He's out of bed and scrambling for his boyfriend who's sound asleep, swaying on his feet, peeing against the door jamb. He pushes him on the shoulder and grabs a towel hanging off the foot of the bed. "Tom, wake up!"

"What? I'm wake. Wha the fuck, Hugh. Go back asleep." All this in sleep-drawl, moist and squishy. Tom stumbles. He's not awake. He tucks his penis into the slit in his boxers and slowly crawls back into bed. He's snoring before he hits the pillow.

Hugh wipes up the mess. He's not even mad. He puts the piss towel in the bathtub down the hall, then walks back to their room, but doesn't go in. He stands in the dim light from the streetlamp coming in through the window and watches Tom's chest rise and fall. It's after midnight. He's wide awake. He thinks about working on his project—he could get another couple of inches done on the cow, or maybe he should start on the calf. He doesn't move. He watches Tom and scratches his chest, feeling alone in the world and unmoored. Not so much lonely as invisible. Hugh's thinking about movies, the colour of loss in movies, or not loss, but absence—that slate blue or staid, matte, dull blue-grey.

The phone rings.

TOM'S GONNA MAKE DAN FRANKLIN PAY

Third time out to Franklin's since February. Shitty breed-ing this year—heifers and big bulls. Tom's had to pull two calves already, one in the middle of a snowstorm, and now a Caesarean. Dan Franklin's favourite word is *motherfucker*.

Tom carries a stiff-bristled plastic brush he uses to wash things—incision sites on the sides of cows, instruments if he drops them, and, once he's done the call and the night is over, he washes the stainless steel bucket and his rubber boots. He's got a system.

Dan Franklin says, "The motherfucker didn't move. I had it nailed. We were out two nights." He spits on the snow. He's talking about hunting deer. "Motherfucker didn't even move."

Tom scrubs the inside of the bucket. He lifts it a little and scrubs vigorously once more around so the hot, soapy water sloshes onto the outside of the bucket. He holds the bucket up high and washes the outside of it, even the bottom, with equal vigour. He gets it shiny clean.

Dan Franklin says, "Didn't think this one'd be so much of a problem. Motherfuckin' big calf, though, boy." He whistles. Fishes a cigarette out of a crumpled pack and ges-tures to Tom with it.

Tom shakes his head. He's busy.

"Motherfuckin' nuisance, man. Got us out here so late." He lights his cigarette, inhales, and aims his stream of smoke at the stars.

Tom stands with his gumboot heels touching and bends at the waist. He gently pours the hot, soapy water onto his boots until only half the water remains in the bucket, and he uses his scrub brush to clean the tops, and then the treads, one by one. He stands on one foot, balancing the bucket out to the side, swiping at the treads with his scrub brush. Both boots scrubbed, he pours the remainder of the water onto the tops of his feet. His boots steam, gleaming green and clean in the yard light and the interior lights from his running Bronco. He admires his work. He's taking his time.

"Goddamn, it's cold out here. Cold as a motherfucker!"

Dan Franklin can't wait all night in the yard, Tom knows. He sets the clean bucket inside the back of his Bronco and puts the brush inside it. He picks up his case and sets it beside the bucket, in front of the two empty water jugs. The calf puller nestles between the seatbacks and pokes out over his equipment in the back. It was a beautiful Caesarean. Almost textbook. Tom is proud of the little time it took him, the small incision, the tidiness of his sutures. He's pleased with how the cow nosed the calf directly after they'd dragged it over to her. He'd seen her licking it as he trudged out of the barn with his gear.

Now, bucket stowed, he looks at Dan Franklin. Dan Franklin knows. Tom knows. Dan takes off his hat and inspects its brim. He knocks imaginary dust off it, slapping it on his leg. Finally he looks at Tom. Tom lets his gaze stay, calm and solid, on Dan's dark eyes.

"My dad said cows and women will cost you. Said never invest in livestock. Said motherfucking cows'll get you every fucking time. Jesus Christ almighty. Fuck. How much do I owe you, Doc?"

"I'll send you the bill in the morning, Dan. Don't be surprised by the after-hours fee. I'll include it in the tally." Tom smiles at him, and hops into the running truck.

Motherfucking make him pay, Tom thinks. It's a short drive back to the clinic with that satisfaction.

Sometimes after midnight, black as the inside of a sheep. Tom with cold hands on the wheel. What if, beyond the puddle of yellow headlights, the world has disappeared? Tom remembers that scene from somewhere, a book, a movie, maybe. The world beyond the headlights gone. The wind shakes the Bronco, pushes it, so he has to hold tight to keep the wheels straight. He feels tiny. Beyond the grey highway and yellow lines and the fence posts he can see every now and then, what if the world breaks off and disappears into space? What if he's driving into space? What if, for some reason, he's the only one left alive? While he was working, between the time he left Frank Early in the yard of his farm with his three collies racing around in the twilight and now, full dark, he's the only man left on earth breathing? Jesus. He's spooked.

He turns on the heat. Right up. Full blast. He watches the yellow line and reaches blind for his toque on the passenger seat. Finds it. Puts it on. Jesus.

What if this is it?

Everything passes in black and white. Dubois' little place there on the curve of Stoney Creek. Blackson Bridge. That hollow where he saw the moose and triplets last spring. All grey and black and white in the moonlight. He peers up through the windshield. Big Dipper. Stars galore. Nothing else. Hair stands up all over his body. Jesus.

What if Hugh is dead? What if he gets back there and Hugh is dead? And Janelle. And the cats in the kennels and all the people in town. Jesus. His stomach clenches. Like he could barf and crap his pants at the same time.

He drives faster, then he slows right down. Then comes to a complete stop in the middle of the highway. No traffic. The wind shakes the Bronco. Clouds race across the black and white sky. Jesus.

He turns on the CBC and cranks the dial to raise the volume over the roar of the heater. Puts his foot on the accelerator. God, let there be life beyond this moment. Let there be Hugh at the end of the road.

Teapot Mountain tenderly licks the sac that used to hold his testicles. He runs his tongue over and over the bag, lining up the hairs, soaking the whole area, scrotum, shaft, penis, with all his love and attention. Every few minutes Janelle nudges him with her foot to make him stop, and he stops. He sits up with his head alert and surveys the room from under the desk at Janelle's legs and shoes, the chair, the garbage can and shredder, and beyond the desk, into the office where the man sits rubbing his temples. Teapot goes back to licking until he feels warm and tired and lays his head down on his paws. He watches the man rock back and forth in his chair rubbing his head and hair. Teapot Mountain can relate—he knows how good it feels to be rubbed. And he knows how good it feels to rub. He sits up. He watches the man and thinks about rubbing. He creeps between Janelle's legs and the edge of the desk and pads over to the man. The man hears his nails on the floor and comes alert. Teapot presents his side to the fellow and leans slightly into him, inviting him to partake in the pleasure of rubbing his sleek fur. Teapot feels warm and sleepy again when the man falls to petting him, fondling his ears, sliding his hand from the nape of Teapot's neck right down to the base of his tail. He lets himself lean harder, until it's too hard to stand, and then he turns four circles and curls up on the fellow's feet. As a kindness.

WHEN DID TOM LAST EAT?

Breakfast, maybe. Yesterday. He didn't have lunch. He was going to, but a dog with a broken leg came in and he amputated mid-thigh. As he sutured and snipped his stitch ends, Tom's mind was occupied with the dog's life after surgery—tripods don't do so badly, if the family cares for them—and it would be a beautiful scar, hardly visible once the hair grew back, just a slight, raised line following the inside curve of the thigh.

He wants macaroni and cheese with crumbled Rip-L Chips on top, baked until the cheddar is gooey. His mum's. He wants macaroni and cheese and a pale ale and for it to be summer already and for Hugh to say yes to walking to the creek after dinner so they can swim. They could laze on the bank and talk about life, the sky, how dragonflies mate.

Janelle reaching in for the mug at his elbow startles him off the microscope. He has no idea what he was looking for or for how long he'd been looking.

"You were sleeping."

"No." He rubs his eye sockets with both fists.

"You didn't move for three quarters of an hour. I did laundry, cleaned kennels, fed the inmates, and you haven't moved. Your tea is cold."

"I had tea?"

Janelle stares heavenward. "There's always tea. I'm always making you tea. You never drink it."

He sees the constellation of empty mugs littering his desktop beyond the microscope. "I don't have time. I start one..."

"And the phone rings. I know."

"Shall I put the kettle on?"

She wipes her bangs off her forehead. "No, it's too late now. It's almost five. I'm going to take Teapot Mountain and walk him with the others in the back, then go home."

Tom closes his eyes. Five o'clock.

"Tom? I left the paperwork for Mrs. Fletcher's cat open on the desk. She's ready to go. And that neuter you were going to do this morning that the amputation pushed back is ready, too. Paperwork under Fletcher's. And there's the billing from last night I need you to look at. I'm not sure what all went on."

He is examining one fingernail very close up. It hurts, but he can't remember why. Redness at the cuticle, not much swelling.

"Tom?"

He looks at her. Really looks. She's strong. A woman who comes to work in her old riding boots with horse hair on her jeans. Local. Who knows the old folks and makes them feel important, when he can't remember their names. He knows where their farms are and their herds' health histories and how long they've been trying whatever scheme it is they are trying, whether feed or breeding or new fencing systems, but he can't remember names. Janelle can. She gets them laughing.

"Tom?" She is two steps closer. Her brown eyes pity him.

He's fine. "Thanks for the prep. I'll handle it all tonight. If I get called out..."

"When you get called out."

He deflates in his chair.

Janelle touches his arm, ever so lightly. "I'll put the kettle on."

TOM'S BRONCO IS NOT WHERE HE LEFT IT

It is hard to pretend like you know what you're doing when you're walking the perimeter of the co-op parking lot for the second time with two bags of groceries and a log of toilet paper rolls under your arm. Tom nods to people he knows. He grins in the fresh wind, under the concrete sky. He notices cobalt blue clouds jamming up on the western horizon and he keeps on walking like he knows where he's going.

Hugh drives up in the Bronco. He rolls down his window and keeps pace with Tom. "You getting some exercise? Doing laps while you wait for me?" He's laughing, but he stops when he meets Tom's eyes. "You forgot, didn't you? I said I'd pick you up. Oh Tommy." He stops and jumps out, leaves the truck running, and jogs around to Tom's side to open the door for him.

HUGH AND TOM, AN INVENTORY

Hugh: broken wrist from skiing, broken toe from kicking a chair, chipped heart from a few old sweethearts.

Tom: broken collarbone, fractured wrist, broken ribs (not sure how many), broken femur (six months out of commission for that one), broken hand from punching a wall, greenstick tibial fracture when he fell out of a tree at six.

Both: broken crock pot, broken screen door, broken vase (by accident), broken popcorn maker (small fire in the kitchen), backward taps in the bathroom sink (that was Tom), broken headlight on the Bronco (Hugh, but no one mentions it).

NINE TIMES OUT OF TEN

Nine times out of ten he's sure of nothing. His dread is like fascia under his skin, making up more of his body than all the fluid inside, than all his organs, than any synapse he honed in university: he is a dummy and he knows it. However, he holds a strange role of judgement: It Is Time For This Medical Intervention, It Is Time For This Drug, We Have Long Passed the Time for Dicking Around... He knows nothing. Imposter Syndrome. Constant and relentless. He might be getting an ulcer. His stomach hurts. He's furious. He's deeply, untreatably sad.

It's because he hasn't eaten.

Tom eats a granola bar. He eats an apple and a wedge of cheese. He drinks the gas station chocolate milk and Eat More bought at his last stop and he closes his eyes and leans his head against the headrest. He waits for the panic to pass.

The Bronco is like a coat he wears. He bought it so cheap. There are holes where rust has eaten through the wheel wells that he patched with plywood. When he corners hard he can hear his case and bucket and jugs slide across the painted board and clang into the truck bed. The front seat is the best seat in the house, he tells himself. It's his throne. He opens his eyes to Hulatt in all its dinky glory and he feels almost okay. Okay enough to check his phone, to call Janelle, to get his marching orders, and move out.

Nine times out of ten it's that he's hungry. Or tired. Or he's forgotten something. That one time out of ten, he doesn't know what it is. Disaster? Act of God.

This, at least, he can do, now that he's eaten: breech calf

at Foster's, twenty kilometres down Braeside Road past the old Rivers place, turn left at the mailbox with a mallard on it. His equipment's in the back. Full tank of gas. Head full of schooling. He's got everything he needs.

HUGH: RUBBING PUPPIES

Hugh says Tom would make a great small animal vet. He says there are practices in the city that would love to have him.

Tom says they'll get to sleep through the night in the summer. They just need to hold on.

Hugh knows some of Tom's skills—he's seen him with cats and budgies, hamsters, and rabbits. He knows Tom is good at his job, that every single thing about an animal interests him—every bone and tendon, the sockets and valves, the cysts and diseases. None of this interests Hugh. Tom says he likes Blackleg the best ("What?" says Hugh). He loves the Latin name of the disease: *Clostridium chauvoei*, the cluck and whisper in the sounds of the words, though Blackleg unchecked can decimate a whole herd.

Hugh tells Tom he loves his job too much. Tom had called him to come over from the house to help him with a dog and her puppies in the clinic. Hugh isn't happy about it. He has to leave his Lego. He says Tom is only half-present in their conversations. He says Tom isn't listening. He says Tom should focus on them more.

"Rub the puppy more," Tom says. It will die if he doesn't. It's late at night, a whelping gone on too long, the bitch struggling until Tom put her under to get the puppies out himself.

"You should open your eyes to us," Hugh says. "There will always be sick cats and hysterical owners. There won't always be today, right now, Tom. Or tomorrow."

Tom comes around the operating table and takes the puppy out of Hugh's hands. He snatches his towel and rubs vigorously. "Like this. Or it will die." The pup starts to wriggle and mewl. Tom tucks it into the warmth of its mother's fur and hands Hugh the towel and another still baby. He gets back to the incision. Two more puppies for sure, but the last one he'd pulled out was soft, decomposing in utero. "We could lose the mother to shock or infection. We don't have a lot of time."

"It's like you can't see beyond this room." Hugh holds the puppy, peering at its tiny ears and closed mouth. "You don't come out for days. And when you do, it's to go out on a call."

"Rub, Hugh. You're its only chance. I can't do this and that both."

"I know," he says. "That's what I'm saying."

DARKNESS OVERCOMES

Tom puts his head down and keeps working. He's not going to look at the corpse in the corner. He's not going to let this get to him. He washes his instruments and keeps his head down. It doesn't matter. It's one calf in hundreds. Stillbirth. No apparent reason. He knows it wasn't his fault.

Tom keeps his head down and sets each metal tool into its place in his case, the needles with the needles, their beautiful, curving hooks and eyes, the scissor clamps with the scissor clamps. He wipes down his bottle of Amoxicillin, the iodine bottle. He wipes off his glasses on his handkerchief, and he does not look at the wet body of the calf in the corner, still steaming, dead. He doesn't think about how it won't ever taste grass or feel the wind ruffling its coat. Shit like this just happens. Cows have other calves, and the mother nosing this one, nudging its dead body to wake it up, make it suck, the mother licking her placenta—it doesn't matter, she's just another cow who'll pine for a calf all season, while all the other calves frolic and the other mothers have their udders eased by nursing. He doesn't think about any of this. He scrubs his knife and his axe. He scrubs his hands and arms, the bristles digging into the cracks in his winter-dry skin, the cracks opening and bleeding thin pink streaks into the hot soapy water. None of it matters.

He washes his instruments. He packs his case. He says, "Someone get that calf out of here," and someone listens. Two of the farmer's sons take a leg each and drag the calf out of the pen to the dark back of the barn. The cow starts lowing and there is an absolute hole in Tom's heart. He can't anymore. He puts the case down.

"Doc, you want to come back to the house for a cup of tea?"

"It's late, Walter." He can't even look up.

"Listen, Judy's been up all the while. She's got the kettle on. It's always on. Listen, it wouldn't put us out. We know what this season's like. The least we can do is offer you tea."

Tom sees the man's hand resting on his arm: the wrinkles in it, the calloused, strength of a farmer, a father, a husband, a self-made man, and he knows he can't.

"I've been up for days, Walter. I can't." Tom stops.

"I hear you," Walter says, but he keeps his hand there. Warm. Warming. "It's a standing offer. Anytime. You come out here anytime and we'll have tea, or coffee, or something stronger. And you bring whoever you want with you. Anytime. You hear, Tom Gunn? I mean it."

HUGH LETS DINNER CONGEAL

He sits on the couch in the window and watches for head-lights coming down the driveway. The ceiling lights are off. He listens to Philip Glass on his phone and sits in the dark and waits for his boyfriend to come home from another farm call. Is he waiting for his future? Is he already in his future and he's fucked it up? Tom's fucking it up. He's wait-ing for Tom and sitting on this grotty chesterfield in a house not of his own choosing with a mess of a project festering in the guest room, and he knows he's made an error—he's in the process of fucking it up—and this is not his future. This is an interim. Nothing so religious as a purgatory, not for Hugh. A bunch of moments strung together on a string. But, he realizes, he holds the string. If he lets even one side of the string go, the beads will fall off the untended end and he will have changed the course of his life. This interim—beef au jus, the au jus (just jus? the gravy) congealing on the countertop, carrots cooked in butter and sugar harden-ing into fatty orange rounds and yellow curds—is like any other interim. Like the summer before university. Like the moment before Paul Dubois leaned in and kissed him. Like the first time Tom said his name, asked him if he could, then touched his face. Like the times during every future calving season when Tom will be out and Hugh will be waiting with some other stupid project on the go, dinner ruined on the table, and no friends in town—the woman at the post office snubbing him again when he picks up a parcel for Tom, the river frozen into man-grinding chunks of ice rushing under the bridge, the black water horrifying. He will always wait. Or he will stop waiting.

Hugh examines his reflection in the window. He is not young. He has crow's feet already and he dyes his hair. He loves his lover's lower lip. He hates the shape of his own nose—the alarming bump in the bridge of it. He has had two residencies in Canada and one in Spain. He has the opportunity of his own life. He has the opportunity of Tom, and he has the opportunity of himself.

Hugh examines the kitchen, lit only by the stove light, and knows he needs to act to end this interim—in order to start another portion of his life, he must drop the string or hold tight. Is this what life would always be like? Waiting, deciding, acting, not acting, waiting. Choosing? He might have made a choice. He has to make a choice.

He swallows. He runs his hands through his hair. He puts his chin on his fist and watches the driveway for headlights. He thinks of Tom's long throat. His future.

JANELLE AND HUGH

Hugh always comes in the clinic's front door, never through the kennel or the large animal clinic entrance. He stomps his boots off on the mat. She'll give him that.

"Hi Hugh." Janelle presses the star and the adding machine clatters with a final tally.

"Hi there." He comes across the waiting room, giving the Donnelly's basset hound a wide berth (Mrs. Donnelly's eyes all over him), and leans on the reception desk. He's got Kleenex residue scrubbed into the stubble over his lip, under his big nostrils. "Seen Tom?"

"Not for hours. He had a call first thing. Backed everyone up." She indicates Mrs. Donnelly with a nod. Hugh nods back.

Cadillac, the clinic cat, hops up onto the reception desk and sallies up to Hugh. He stands back so she can't reach him. Janelle scoops her up and holds her in her lap, stroking her tortoiseshell fur, feels her begin to purr. "What are you up to? Wanna come back for a hot drink?"

Hugh shakes his head. He could smile. Janelle thinks he'd be handsome if he shaved more often. And if he smiled. Despite his nostrils. "No, it's okay. I've got something on the go. Just tell Tom I stopped by, okay?"

She doesn't say anything. He's waiting, but she doesn't want to say anything or nod or smile or do anything for him. She didn't even want to make him a drink, but she would've if he'd wanted one. For Tom. She watches Hugh give up and make his way out of the room, keeping close to the unused chairs on the perimeter. She'll do whatever it takes for Tom, but she doesn't have to do a thing for Hugh.

One text from Janelle, two from Hugh.

Hugh's says: *Eggs or beans on toast?* and, less than a second later: *How the mighty fall.*

Janelle's says: *Did u use two ampules of freezing at Jones' last night or what? Full cost for C-section plus after hours? Answer quick. Billing.*

Tom sits on the hood of the Bronco in delicious spring sunshine less than five kilometres east of the Stellako River Bridge. He's got his phone in one hand and a poorly rolled cigarette in the other. The lucky thing is he's in a rare pocket of cell service on the highway. The unlucky thing is he's out of gas.

He contemplates the cigarette and feels his phone buzz. He puts it on the hood of the truck beside him and fishes a lighter out of the plastic bag in his lap. It's new. The tobacco, too. If he hadn't been so intent on buying his first pack ever of tobacco, he might have remembered to fill up. Instead he'd made note, the night before, of the old uncle at the auction yard leisurely rolling a smoke and how he wanted to do that, too. Rationalized it might keep him awake while driving. Then he made his attempt at rolling one and realized all those cowboys in movies were only pretending to be buckaroos rolling a dart in one hand, the reins of a horse in the other. Liars. Tom, whose sutures disappear like magic, like God himself had zapped an incision closed, rolls a cigarette like a dolt; tobacco weeps out the crinkled, flaccid end of it, and the roll so loose, he isn't sure it will light or stay lit.

He has plenty of time to find out.

His phone buzzes again, sending a tinny, harmonic rattle up into the air. Tom flicks the lighter and brings the flame to the cigarette at his lips and inhales. Nothing happens, but he decides to sit back as if his cigarette is lit and he's enjoying it. It's kind of funny. He fake puffs, fake exhales. His phone buzzes.

He could walk to Fort Fraser. It wouldn't take long. And Lord knows he's waved at three farmers he knows already. It probably wouldn't be hard to get a ride.

Tom takes another pretend puff. Lets it out. Then he curls his paw around the smoke and tries to light it again. He sucks in hard, coughs, sucks in, coughs and coughs, then flicks the light again and it's going. He inhales, not too hard, aware he's tender-lunged, that he's doing himself damage, and he's smoking. Like a sailor, he imagines. Sitting on his truck hood, watching the birds going crazy in the marsh beside the highway. Watching the clouds rush past the mountain. Watching the trucks zip by on the highway.

His phone buzzes. He squints at it, a black cloud of tobacco trapped in his lungs, dread in his heart. Hugh. He breathes out and reads:

I love you Tommy
happy bday, big boy

His cigarette is out when he sucks on it. He flicks it into the ditch like an old-time cowboy, sunshine all over him.

Hugh and Janelle join forces, just this once. They work together. Tom's been gone for too long. They take Janelle's Pathfinder, Teapot Mountain in the passenger seat, Hugh in the back, and they find Tom on the highway. His Bronco, pulled off on the shoulder, seems abandoned and dead. The headlights illuminate a corona of hair on the far side of the vehicle. Did he crash? Did he go through the windshield? Hugh yells, bangs on her seat to make her stop, and is out of the truck before she's put it in park. He's screaming *Are you dead? Tom, are you dead?* But Tom pops his head up over the roof of the vehicle and squints in the light.

"Hugh!" he shouts, and with such delight.

Hugh runs around the vehicle. Janelle stands at the open driver's side door, Teapot whining at her ear. She waits. Through the back window, the front windscreen, and across the length of the vehicle, she sees the men embrace. Hugh hauls Tom down off the truck, a packet of tobacco falls unnoticed in the dirt, and they hug and Hugh punches Tom in the arm, and Tom yells *I ran out of gas* so many times.

Hugh had stopped her in the driveway. She'd been about to lock the clinic and go up to the house to check in, which she never did, but she hadn't heard from Tom in ages. Hugh had been this close to calling the cops. Hugh didn't have a car, so they took her Pathfinder.

New moon and frost. A typical March day where they'd had snow in the morning, bright sun all afternoon, a total thaw, and then a freeze-up as soon as night fell. They'd driven in scared silence, in the near-dark, each reaching out to him—Janelle feeling forward along the highway, familiar with each rise and turn, Hugh blind and dumb to the land-scape, terror-stricken, undone. Teapot Mountain sat tall and unperturbed in the passenger seat, going for a car-ride, the long spring dusk unfolding around them.

"You scared us," Janelle says, when the men come close enough to hear her. Hugh thinks she sounds accusing. Tom hears love.

The men clamber in the back and the dog assumes his customary position in the passenger seat. Janelle drives them back to town while Tom tells his tale, the empty gas tank, the early dark, how no one stopped though he saw people he knew all day, everyone raising a finger off the steering wheel, or a hand, in greeting.

Janelle drives right to the Lucky Dragon restaurant. They drink Caesars and laugh. Janelle and Hugh are familiar each with the others' lives, but only the surface, only the re-cent past, only in that they share the same square kilometre every day and a confounding love for the skinny, tired man they've just rescued off the highway. They love his forgetful-ness and his care. They can't get over how kind he is even to snakes. They both know that deep down he loves Teapot Mountain more thoroughly than he loves either of them.

That night Tom vomits up sweet and sour pork in a vivid orange stream—food poisoning or an adverse reaction to red dye number five. Hugh rubs his back, then brings him mint tea and they stay up, not talking, until Tom is done his tea and falls asleep. That night Hugh dismantles four and a half feet of brown Lego that might once have become a larger-than-life facsimile of a cow. He puts each brick back in the box it came in. Decides to donate all the boxes to the church thrift store before he leaves town.

THEN, WHEN WINTER'S OVER

Though he is careful not to say it out loud or he'll invite a squall, in the sunshine, sitting on the hood of his Bronco, between calls, barely in cell range, tobacco bunched in his fist, the traffic roaring past at one truck per minute, Tom is still. It feels like the first time in months. He has two days of paperwork backed up on his desk, Teapot Mountain likely asleep underneath. He lost a toque at Romano's the other night, after a particularly sweaty call where he and three men wrestled a live bull calf from its half-dead mother. His cell phone has two bars and two percent power. He has a bottle of water and an emergency granola bar in his console. He has seven years of university education, two years and four months of practice under his belt. He has zero hope for better years than this. He's glad he painted the ceiling of the large animal clinic sky blue—it gives him hope. He may paint a sun up there in the future.

He feels the air on his skin, and after so many months of barn coats and darkness, it feels better than any memory of air on skin he can conjure—better even than spring break in Mexico when he was fifteen, better than chopping wood, building up steam, then ripping off his shirt to sweat in fresh air. He hoards the freshness and weak sunlight on his skin, sucking it into him in advance of next year's chill, in anticipation of this career chock-full of discomfort.

He inspects his hands. He rubs his elbows. He will have arthritis, for sure. He will be kicked in the knees by horses and bit when he's floating their teeth. He will have scars from cuts and nicks and nips and falls. He will break ribs while semen-collecting in the chute at the auction. He will have neck pain from whiplash from car crashes he hasn't had yet. He will fall asleep at the wheel. Janelle will wash out a bite wound on his arm and one on his hand and another on his calf. He will buy her flowers when she miscarries the baby of a rodeo clown she falls for. He will visit her bedside when she gives birth to a live baby girl six years and five dogs from now, and he will be that baby's godparent. He will owe the bank for twenty-two years, and then one day he'll get the notice he owns his land outright and his practice too. He will sit back. He will find a cold cup of tea at his elbow. He will stroke the fur of Cadillac the Second and listen to him purr in the empty, after-hours clinic, and he will smile.

HUGH BRINGS TOM A SANDWICH

Hugh brings Tom a sandwich. Tells Tom he's leaving. They both cry. Hugh drinks both beers.

POSTSCRIPT: TOM GUNN, DVM

Once, in the middle of it, some years in, a conservation officer brings in an otter. His plan is for Tom to put a GPS tracker in the otter. The old Doc had done it twice before to other otters, but they'd lost track of them once they got back in the wild, whether because they died and the trackers were lost or for some reason the machinery stopped working.

It's mid-February. Tom has a cold sore and a runny nose. He last slept through the night in January. He loves this opportunity—the chance to dig his hands past the coarse waterproof guardhairs into the soft, thick underfur of the otter, a wild animal, to help the conservation officer do his job. He says *of course I'll do it*, but then he sees the tracker: a metal tube two inches in diameter and six inches long. *It'll kill it*, he thinks. And he wants to stop. All of it. He wants to never interfere in the lives of animals again. But the otter, the whole great length of it, its webbed feet and tiny ears, this sleek brown life, is stretched out on his operating table, and the C.O. is there, describing where he should insert the machine, asking how long will the animal be out, telling him the story again of where they'd trapped it, what the terrain was like, in every word the thrill of a wildlife manager achieving a scientific objective.

Tom strokes the animal's fur. He runs his eyes over the closed lids of the otter, remembers the weight of it as the two of them hefted it, unconscious, out of the trap, onto the table. Its tail is a magnificent whip. He wishes Hugh could see the otter's fur—there are a million shades of brown in the brown; the bright, operating room light picks up every hue.

The C.O. is enthusiastic. He lives in town. He has red-bone coonhounds, three of them. Three little girls and his wife is a pilot. Tom vaccinated all three hounds when they were pups and every member of the family had come, like it was a major event—ensuring the health of the copper-eyed puppies, each one with five humans and two dogs who would miss the shit out of it if it died.

In the marshland north of Fort St. James this otter had a den, possibly a mate, possibly kits, or brothers and sisters, a territory of intricate waterways, creeks and runnels and ponds where it gobbled fish and frogs, swam alongside dragonfly larvae. It could smell its way home. Tom strokes its fur and feels dread like he's standing in river water, the cold seeping upward into his bones. He'll do it, he'll put the tracker in, and the otter will die.

Each year as summer starts in earnest he gets a postcard from somewhere in the world with cows on it, real or cartoon, wearing great, huge bells in Switzerland, or bulls with massive balls hanging in stretched sacs past their pointy hocks. It's all the Hugh he gets, in the end, and it isn't enough, but it's kind of nice—a joke his former lover has with himself, that he shares with Tom and that verges on regret. Hugh with his long lashes and yearning. Hugh lit from behind, in silhouette in the kitchen, his features invisible from the driveway, his despair flashing like a lightless beacon, out past Tom in his dirty coverall and boots into a cold, spring night.

Tom pins each postcard on top of the other as they come, though not the last one—a photo postcard of Hugh and a big man with long brown curls, their arms around a Scottish Highland cow, whose messy hair hides its expression. This one he lets disappear among the papers and vet journals that cover his desk, never looks at it again, though Janelle may well have seen it, and likely filed it where it belonged.

Tom Gunn will treat otters and eagles and owls and snakes, turtles, budgies, a parrot and two types of guinea pig in his career. He'll own odd animals and treat each one he owns for something at some point, and some will survive—most notably Lacey, who died of old age at twenty-seven. Tom finds her in the calf pen, stiff in the corner, while the year's new calves bunt and buck around the pen. Along with the cattle, pigs, goats, horses and sheep, he'll treat domestic and exotic animals and love every challenge offered him. And once, he'll operate on the glass-eyed stuffed bear of his goddaughter while she stands on a stool in his operating room, the both of them in scrubs, masks and caps. Janelle, alternately trash-talking him and cheering them on.

It won't be easy, and some of it nearly kills him. But it is interesting. And sometimes in the straw and shit of a barnyard there is grace. Sometimes in the operating room. Sometimes in winter, sometimes in summer, and always at the turn of the year in March, when calving season winds down to nothing and he finds sleep again. And dreams.

Tom looks the conservation operator in the eye. He smiles at the man. He puts the GPS tracker in the otter. It dies less than a day later of shock. In the sorrow, a flicker of anticipation for the autopsy.

ACKNOWLEDGEMENTS

Vet medicine is demanding, sorrowful, inspiring and horrifying, sometimes all at once—and these stories are part of my effort to understand growing up near my dad's rural vet practice, close to life and death, which gave me a massive respect for the tender and thoughtful way he negotiated both. I am more grateful than I can say for his making us part of his work-life and for explaining everything along the way. Equally, compassion and patience were demanded of my mum as she waited by the window for his headlights to turn in the driveway. My parents are not in this book—the characters are all invented—but there are aspects of them here. That love is careful stitching, reading aloud, bookkeeping, storytelling, and silence, that love is handmade: I am grateful to Walter and Judy Wigmore for showing me this and for teaching me to look.

The real spaces and sideways memories in the book I offer to James, Susie, and David Wigmore, who shared my strange and lovely childhood. I would have included Lydia, Lady, Scamper, Waggles, Nosy Hot Pussy, Teeny, and all the others, but there wasn't room enough.

I grew up and live, and these stories were written, on the traditional territories of the Dakehl, the Lheidli T'enneh, and the Saik'uz Peoples—I am grateful and lucky to consider these places home. To friends and farmers in Vanderhoof, Fort St James, and in all the outlying communities, who made us welcome after a farm call even if we were a pack of wild hooligans, and let us into their kitchens and sometimes even gave us cookies, I send out my hellos.

Thanks to Invisible, to Julie Wilson, Bryan Ibeas, and Megan Fildes, and to the tireless and brilliant Leigh Nash who asks the hardest questions, says yes at just the right times, who sees where I'm going, and who helps me get there.

"Love, Ramona" is for David Arthurs. Twelve to seventeen would have been unbearable without him. "Bare Limbs in Summer Heat" has at its centre a snippet of a poem by Tomas Transtromer, translated by Robin Robertson: *Love's drama has died down, and they're sleeping now,/ but their dreams will meet as colours meet/ and bleed into each other/ in the dampened pages of a child's painting-book* (from "The Couple," *The Deleted World*, 2011). "Night Watch" is dedicated to Karen and Cindy, best friends and best animal health technicians (and their dogs), who made us welcome, who kept our dad safe, who didn't kick us out as often as we deserved. Deep thanks to Dennis Lee for the epigraph, whose words are a throughline, who brought me to song.

I'm grateful to all early readers of the book including the League of Extraordinary Women.

Finally, I wish there was an adequate way to say thank you to Travis, Elly, and Emmett Sillence for their thoughts and love and company, in the wilderness and out. Let this suffice: Heart.

INVISIBLE PUBLISHING produces fine Canadian literature for those who enjoy such things. As an independent, not-for-profit publisher, our work includes building communities that sustain and encourage engaging, literary, and current writing.

Invisible Publishing has been in operation for over a decade. We released our first fiction titles in the spring of 2007, and our catalogue has come to include works of graphic fiction and non-fiction, pop culture biographies, experimental poetry, and prose.

We are committed to publishing diverse voices and experiences. In acknowledging historical and systemic barriers, and the limits of our existing catalogue, we strongly encourage writers from LGBTQ2SIA+ communities, Indigenous writers, and writers of colour to submit their work.

Invisible Publishing is also home to the Bibliophonic series of music books and the Throwback series of CanLit reissues.

If you'd like to know more, please get in touch: info@invisiblepublishing.com